Burney's Laugh & Other Stories of Stacy Aumonier

Stacy Aumonier was born at Hampstead Road near Regent's Park, London on 31st March 1877.

He came from a family with a strong and sustained tradition in the visual arts; sculptors and painters.

On leaving school it seemed the family tradition would also be his career path. In particular his early talents were that of a landscape painter. He exhibited paintings at the Royal Academy in the early years of the twentieth century.

In 1907 he married the international concert pianist, Gertrude Peppercorn, at West Horsley in Surrey. A year later Aumonier began a career in a second branch of the arts at which he enjoyed a short but outstanding success—as a stage performer writing and performing his own sketches.

The Observer newspaper commented that "...the stage lost in him a real and rare genius, he could walk out alone before any audience, from the simplest to the most sophisticated, and make it laugh or cry at will."

In 1915, Aumonier published a short story 'The Friends' which was well received (and was subsequently voted one of the 15 best stories of 1915 by the Boston Magazine, Transcript).

Despite his age in 1917 at age 40 he was called up for service in World War I. He began as a private in the Army Pay Corps, and then transferred as a draughtsman in the Ministry of National Service.

By now he had four books published—two novels and two books of short stories—and his occupation is recorded with the Army Medical Board as 'author.'

In the mid-1920s, Aumonier received the shattering diagnosis that he had contracted tuberculosis. In the last few years of his life, he would spend long spells in various sanatoria, some better than others.

Shortly before his death, Stacy Aumonier sought treatment in Switzerland, but died of the disease in Clinique La Prairie at Clarens beside Lake Geneva on 21st December 1928. He was 55.

Index of Contents

After breakfast was a good time. Throughout the day there was no moment when his vitality rose to such heights as it did during the first puffs of that early cigar. He would stroll out then into the conservatory, and the bright color of the azaleas would produce in him a strange excitement. His senses would seem sharpened, and he would move quickly between the flowers, and would discuss minor details of their culture with Benyon, the gardener. Then he would stroll through the great spaces of his reception-rooms with his head bent forward. The huge Ming pot on its ebony stand would seem to him companionable and splendid, the Majolica placques which he had bought at Padua would glow serenely. He would go up and feast his eyes on the Chinese lacquer cabinet on its finely wrought gilt base, and his lips would quiver with a tense enjoyment as he lingered by the little carved Japanese ivories in the recess. Above all, he liked to stand near the wall and gaze at the Vandyke above the fireplace. It looked well in the early morning light, dignified and impressive.

All these things were his. He had fought for them in the arena of the commercial world. He had bought them in the teeth of opposition. And they expressed him, his sense of taste, his courage, his power, his relentless tenacity, the qualities that had raised him above his fellows to the position he held. The contemplation of them produced in him a curious, vibrant exhilaration. Especially was this so in the morning when he rose from the breakfast-table and lighted his first cigar.

The great hall, too, satisfied his quivering senses. The walnut paneling shone serenely, and brass and pewter bore evidence that the silent staff whom his housekeeper controlled had done their work efficiently. It was early, barely nine o'clock, but he knew that in the library Crevace and Dilgerson, his private secretaries, would be fidgeting with papers and expecting him. He would keep them waiting another ten minutes while he gratified this clamorous proprietary sense. He would linger in the drawing-room, with its long, gray panels and splendid damask hangings, and touch caressingly the little groups of statuary. The unpolished satinwood furniture appealed to some special esthetic appetite. It was an idea of his own. It seemed at once graceful and distinguished.

He seemed to have so little time during the rest of the day to feel these things. And if he had the time, the satisfaction did not seem the same, for this was the hour when he felt most virile.

In the library the exultation that he had derived from these esthetic pleasures would gradually diminish. It is true that Dilgerson had prepared the rough draft of his amendment to the new Peasant Allotment Bill, and it was an amendment that he was intensely interested in, for if it passed, it might lead to the overthrow of Chattisworth, and that would be a very desirable thing; but nevertheless his interests would flag.

He had a fleeting vision of a great triumph in the House, and himself the central figure. He settled down to discuss the details with Dilgerson. Dilgerson was a very remarkable person. He had a genius for putting his finger on the vital spot of a bill, and he had, moreover, an unfathomable memory. But gradually the discussion of involved financial details with Dilgerson would tire him. He would get restless and say:

"Yes, yes. All right, Dilgerson; put it your own way."

He turned aside to the table where Crevace, coughing nervously, was preparing some sixty-odd letters for him to sign. A charming young man Crevace, with gentle manners and a great fund of concentration. He was the second son of Emma, Countess of Waddes. He had not the great ability of Dilgerson, but he was conscientious, untiring, and very useful.

He discussed the letters and a few social matters with Crevace, while Dilgerson prepared the despatch-case for the cabinet meeting at twelve o'clock.

At half-past eleven a maid entered and brought him a raw egg beaten up with a little neat brandy, in accordance with custom.

He told her that Hervieu, the chauffeur, need not come for him. He would walk over to Downing Street with Mr. Dilgerson. As a matter of fact, there was still one or two points upon which he was not quite clear about the rights of rural committees. Dilgerson had made a special study of these questions. It was a great temptation to rely more and more on Dilgerson.

He enjoyed a cabinet meeting. He felt more at home there than in the House. He liked the mixture of formality and urbanity with which the most important affairs were discussed. He liked to sit there and watch the faces of his fellow-ministers. They were clever, hard-headed men—men who, like himself, had climbed and climbed and climbed. They shared in common certain broad political principles, but he did not know what was at the back of any one of their minds. It amused him to listen to Brodray elaborating his theories about the Peasant Allotment Bill, and enunciating commendable altruistic principles. He knew Brodray well. He was a good fellow, but he did not really believe what he was saying. He had another ax to grind, and he was using the Peasant Allotment Bill as a medium. The divagations of "procedure" were absorbing. It was on the broad back of "procedure" that the interests of all were struggling to find a place. It was the old parliamentary hand who stood the best chance of finding a corner for his wares, the man who knew the ropes. He, too, had certain ambitions.

It seemed strange to look back on. He had been in political affairs longer than he dared contemplate—two distinct decades. He had seen much happen. He had seen youth and ambition ground to powder in the parliamentary machine. He had seen careers cut short by death or violent social scandal. Some men were very foolish—foolish and lacking in moral fiber. That must be it. Moral fiber, the strength not to overstep the bounds, to keep passion and prejudice in restraint, like hounds upon a leash, until their veins became dried and atrophied, and they lacked the desire to race before the wind.

He had done that. And now he sat there in the somber room, among the rustling papers, and the greatest minister of them all was speaking to him, asking his opinion, and listening attentively to his answers. He forced himself to a tense concentration on the issue. He spoke quietly, but well. He remembered all the points that the excellent Dilgerson had coached him in. He was aware of the room listening to him attentively. He knew they held the opinion that he was safe, that he would do the best thing in the interest of the party.

O'Bayne spoke after that, floridly, with wild dashes of Celtic fun; and they listened to him, and were amused, but not impressed. O'Bayne, too, had an ax to grind, but he showed his hand too consciously. He did not know the ropes.

As the meeting broke up, Brodray came up to him and said:

"Oh, by the way, you know I'm dining with you to-night. May I bring my young nephew with me? He 's a sub, in town on a few days' leave."

Of course he smiled and said it would be delightful. What else was it possible to say?

As a matter of fact, he would rather not have had the young sub. He had arranged a small bachelors' dinner,—just eight of them,—and he flattered himself that he had arranged it rather skilfully. There was to be Brodray; and Nielson, the director of the biggest agricultural instrument works in the country; Lanyon, the K. C.; Lord Bowel of the Board of Trade; Tippins, a big landowner from the North; Sir Andrew Griggs, the greatest living authority on the land laws (he had also written a book on "artificial manures"); and Sir Gregory Caste, director of the Museum of Applied Arts.

The latter he felt would perhaps be a little out of it with the rest, but he would help to emphasize his own aspect of social life, its irreproachable taste, and patronage of the arts. It would be a very eclectic dinner-party, and one in which the fusion of the agricultural interests might tend to produce certain opinions and information of use in conducting the Peasant Allotment Bill, and a red-faced young sub dumped into the middle of it would be neither appropriate nor desirable. There was, however, nothing to be done. He and Brodray had always been great friends; that is to say, they had always worked hand in hand.

He rested in the afternoon, for, as the years advanced, he found this more and more essential. There were the strictest instructions left that in no circumstances was he to be disturbed till half-past four. In the meanwhile the egregious Dilgerson would cope with his affairs.

At half-past four he rose, bathed his face, and, after drinking a cup of tea, rejoined his secretaries in the library. In his absence many matters had developed. There was a further accumulation of correspondence, and a neat type-written list of telephone-messages and applications for appointments. There was no flurry about Dilgerson; everything was in order, and the papers arranged with methodical precision.

He lighted his second cigar of the day and sat down. The graceful head of Crevace was inclined over the papers, and the suave voice of Dilgerson was saying:

"I see, sir, that Chattisworth has been speaking up in Gaysfield. Our agent has written; he thinks it might be advisable for you to go up north and explain to your constituents our attitude toward the bill. They must not be—er—neglected for long in these restless times."

Yes, there was something satisfying in this. The sense of power, or, rather, the sense of being within the power focus, the person who understood, who knew what power meant, and yet was great enough to live outside it. Strange why to-day he should be so introspective, why things should appear so abstract! He had a curious feeling as though everything were slipping away, or as though he were seeing himself and his setting from a distance.

He gazed at Dilgerson, with his square chin and his neat mustache, deftly stowing papers into a file while he spoke. He momentarily envied Dilgerson, with his singular grip on life. He was so intense, so sure.

"Yes, yes," he said after a time, "we 'd better go up there, Dilgerson. As you say, they get restless. You might draft me a rough summary of Chattisworth's points. Let me know what you would suggest—precedents, historical parallels, and so on. It is true; they soon get restless."

A feeling of apathy came to him after a time, and he left his secretaries and strolled out into the Mall. A fine rain was drifting from the south, and the tops of the winter trees seemed like a band of gauze veiling the buildings of Whitehall. He went into St. James's Park, and watched the pale lights from the government buildings. Some soldiers, passed him, and a policeman touched his hat.

Usually these things moved him with a strange delight. They were the instruments of power, the symbols of the world he believed in. But to-night the vision of them only filled him with an unaccountable melancholy. He suddenly remembered a day when he had strolled here with his wife twenty-five years ago.

He passed his hand across his brow and tried to brush back a certain memory; but it would not be denied. It was a gray day like this. She had made some remark, something sentimental and entirely meretricious. He remembered vividly that he had chided her at the time. One must not think like that; one must restrain and control these emotional impulses. They are retrograde, destroying. He had succeeded, risen to the position he held, because he had always been master of himself.

After his wife's death it had been easier to do this. His two daughters had married well, one to the Bishop of St. Lubin, and the other to Viscount Chesslebeach, a venerable, but well-informed, gentleman who had been loyal to the party. His son was now in India, holding a position of considerable responsibility. He was free—free to live and struggle for his great ambitions. He was fortunate in that respect; in fact, he had always been fortunate.

He made his way back across the muddy pathway of the Mall imbued with a sudden uncontrollable desire for light and warmth.

Gales met him in the hall and relieved him of his coat. There was an undeniable sense of comfort and security about Gales. He glanced furtively at the ponderous figure of his head-man, who had been with him now longer than he could remember. He muttered something about the inclemency of the weather, and it soothed him to note the ingratiating acquiescence of the servant, as though by addressing him he had conferred a great benefit upon him. He heard the heavy breathing of Gales as he bustled away with his hat and coat, and then he warmed his hands by the fire, and strolled up-stairs to dress.

As he entered his bedroom an indefinable feeling of dreariness came over him again. It was very silent there, and the well-modulated lights above the dressing-table revealed his gleaming silver brushes and the solid properties of the mahogany bed. He looked at the fire and lighted a cigarette, a very unusual habit for him. Then he went into his dressing-room, and noted his clothes all neatly laid out for him and the brass can of hot water wrapped in the folds of a rough towel. The door, half open, revealed the silver rails and taps in the bath-room, and a very low hum of sound suggested a distant power-station or the well-oiled machinery of a lift. It was all wonderfully ordered, wonderfully coordinated.

He strolled from one room to the other on the thick-pile carpet, trying to thrust back the waves of dejection that threatened to envelop him.

At last he threw his cigarette away, and, disrobing himself, washed and dressed.

He felt better then, a little more alert and interested. He turned down the light and went down-stairs. He felt suddenly curiously nervous and apprehensive about the dinner-party. He went into the dining-room and found Gales instructing a new butler in the subtleties of his profession. The table was laid for nine, and indeed looked worthy of Gales and of himself. There was a certain austerity and distinction about the three bowls of red tulips that were placed at intervals along it, and the old silver and the Nuremburg glasses and the cunning arrangements of concealed lights emphasized his own sure taste and discrimination. Nevertheless, he felt nervous. He fussed about the table, and took the champagne-bottles from their ice beds to satisfy himself that Gales had brought up the right year. He fidgeted with one of the type-written menu-cards, and told Gales that on a previous occasion Fouchet had overdone the chopped olives in the Hollandaise. He must speak to him. He was not sure that Fouchet was not going off. His eyesight was failing, or he was becoming careless. The straw potatoes served with the pheasant had been cut too thick, and the savories were apt to be too dry. Gales listened to these criticisms with a lugubrious sympathy, and, bowing, left the room to convey them to the chef.

After that he retired to the small Japanese room on the ground floor. When he had a bachelor party he preferred to receive his guests there. There was something about the black walls and the grotesquely carved fireplace and the heavily timbered ceiling, also carved, and painted dark red, that appealed to his sense of appropriateness in a man's dinner-party. It was essentially a man's room, a little foreboding and bizarre. It symbolized also his appreciation of a race who were above all things clever, clever and patient, industrious, esthetic, with some quality that excited the mystic tendencies of the cultivated Westerner.

He had not long to wait before two of his guests arrived, Sir Gregory Caste and Lansdon the K. C. They had met in the cloak-room, and, having previously made each other's acquaintance at an hotel at Baden-Baden, were discussing the medical values of rival Bavarian springs. It was a subject on which he himself was no mean authority. The conversation had not progressed far before Lord Bowel was shown in. He was a very big man, with a heavy dome of a head, large, pathetic eyes, and a thick, gray beard. He shook hands solemnly without any gleam of welcome, and immediately gave an account of an incurable disease from which his sister was suffering.

Tippins then arrived, a square-headed North-countryman, who did not speak all the evening except in self-defense, and he was followed by Sir Andrew Griggs and Nielson. Sir Andrew was well into the eighties, and Nielson was a thin, keen-faced man with very thick glasses. There was a considerable interval before Brodray arrived with his nephew. They were at least ten minutes late, and Brodray was very profuse with apologies.

It was curious that the young man was almost precisely as he had pictured him. He was just a red-faced boy in khaki. He fancied that Brodray introduced him as "Lieutenant Burney," but he was not sure. It was, in any case, some such name, something ordinary and insignificant.

They then all adjourned to the dining-room without breaking the general level of their conversation, and sat down.

On his right he had Lord Bowel, and on his left Sir Andrew Griggs. Brodray faced him, with Sir Gregory Caste on his right and his nephew on the left. Lanyon sat next to the lieutenant and Nielson and Tippins occupied the intervening spaces. He had thought this arrangement out with considerable care.

It was not until the sherry and caviar had fulfilled their destiny that Lord Bowel managed to complete the full description of his sister's disease. He spoke very slowly and laboriously, and moved his beard with a curious rotary movement as he masticated his food.

Sir Andrew Griggs then managed to break into the conversation with a dissertation on the horrors of being ill in a foreign hotel. He had once been suddenly seized with a serious internal trouble and had had to undergo an operation in an hotel in Zermatt. It was very trying, and the hotel people were very unreasonable.

Brodray sang the praises of a new American osteopathist during the removal of the soup-plates, and the salmon found the director of the National Museum of Applied Arts dilating upon the virtues of grape-fruit as a breakfast food.

The host was in no hurry. He knew that the course of events would be bound to draw the conversation into channels connected with matters that were of moment to the construction of the Peasant Allotment Bill.

What more natural than that the virtues of grape-fruit should lead to the virtues of fresh air and exercise, and then obviously to horse-flesh. At the first glass of champagne the company was already in the country. Horses and dogs! Ah, how difficult to eliminate them from the conversation of a party of representative Englishmen!

Lord Bowel was the first to express his views upon the bill. The conversation led to it quite naturally at the arrival of the pheasant. They were better cooked tonight, and the potatoes were thinner, more refined.

He watched the curious movement of Lord Bowel's beard as he bit the pheasant and said in his sepulchral voice:

"The Groynes amendment will, in my opinion, inflict a grave injustice on the agricultural classes. You may remember that in Gangway's Rural Housings Bill, in eighteen-ninety-five, Lord Pennefy, who was then on the treasury bench, said—"

The ball had started. He had a curious feeling that he wished Dilgerson were there. Dilgerson had such a remarkable memory. He particularly wanted to get Lanyon's views. Lanyon had a great reputation among the people he knew. Unfortunately, he was not a good party man. They said of him that he had a mind like a double-edged sword. He was keen, analytical, and recondite, and he did not mind whom he struck. The lawyer was intently listening to Lord Bowel. His skin was dry and cracked into a thousand little crevices, his cheek-bones stood out, and his cold, abstract eyes were gazing through his rimless pince-nez at his empty glass, for he did not drink.

Lord Bowel dwelt at great length on the bill's unfortunate attitude toward the agricultural laborer, and at even greater length on the probable result of that attitude upon the agricultural laborer at the polls. When he mentioned the party he sank his voice to a lower key, and spoke almost humanly.

The pheasants had disappeared, and little quails in aspic had quivered tremulously in the center of large plates, surrounded by a vegetable salad the secret of which he himself had discovered when living in Vienna, before Lanyon entered the arena with a cryptic utterance, quoting from an Act of James H. He spoke harshly and incisively, like a judge arraigning a criminal. It was very interesting, for the host became aware that as Lanyon proceeded he was not speaking from conviction. He had heard that Lanyon had ambitions of a certain legal position. The bill would not affect it one way or the other, but his reputation as a dialectician must be established beyond question. He had his game to play, too.

Nielson broke in, and seemed to the host to agree with Lord Bowel in an almost extravagant manner. He, too, spoke feelingly when the party was the theme. It was said that Lord Bowel was the power behind the chief. He certainly exerted a great influence in the selection of office-holders. Men whose political reputation was not made invariably agreed with Lord Bowel, in any case before his face.

The game pursued its normal course; the even tenor of the men's voices sounded one long drone of abstract, passionless sound. Under the influence of the good wine and the solemn procession of cunningly arranged foods, they sank into a detached unity of expression. They looked at one another tolerantly, listening for signs and omens, and measuring the value of one another's remarks. There was no enthusiasm, no passion, nothing to belie the suave and cultivated accents of their voices. They seemed, perhaps, unreal to one another, merely a segregation of ideas meeting in a mirage, without prejudice or bias or any great desire for personal expression.

It was as the savory was being removed that young Burney laughed. The host did not catch what it was that made him laugh, neither did he ever know. It was probably some mildly humorous remark of Tippins. But it came crashing through the room like the reel of pipes in a desert. It was not a boisterously loud laugh, but it was loud enough to rise above the general din. It was the quality of it that seemed to rend the air like an electric thrill. It was clear, mellow, vibrant, and amazingly free. It rang out with an unrestrained vibrato of enjoyment. It hung in the air and satisfied its purpose; it seemed to lash the walls of the room and hurl its message defiantly at the ceiling. It could not be subdued, and it could never be forgotten. It was an amazing laugh. It was like the wind on the moors or the crash of great, high waves breaking on a rock, something that had been imprisoned and suddenly breaks free and rides serenely to its end.

And the saintly Cybeline—

It was curious. Why, immediately he heard the young man's laugh, did this line occur to him? Gales was standing by the sideboard looking flustered and perturbed. People did not laugh in the presence of Gales. He had a faculty of discouraging any flippant digressions from the dignity of politics or dinner. Lanyon was looking in the young man's direction, his keen eyes surveying the wine-glasses set there.

Old Sir Andrew looked at him also and smiled dimly; but, surprisingly enough, the others hardly seemed to have noticed the laugh.

Lord Bowel was saying:

"If, therefore, we are prepared to accept this crisis which the opposition, with a singular lack of insight, in my opinion, seem disposed to precipitate upon the country, we shall be—er—lacking in loyalty not only to the—er—Constitution, but to ourselves, and I said to the chief on Wednesday—"

And the saintly Cybeline—

What on earth did it mean? What was Lord Bowel talking about? Why did the young man's laugh still seem to be ringing round the room? He looked at him; the boy was talking animatedly to Brodray and grinning; he thought he caught something about "we did n't sleep under cover for a fortnight." He had not been drinking, certainly not to excess. No one had had sherry except the silent Tippins. He might have had three glasses of champagne. It certainly did n't account for the laugh; besides, it was not that sort of laugh.

"There was something, something something.
And the something will entwine,
And the something, something, something
With the saintly Cybeline.

A shadowy vision glimmered past the finger-bowl in front of him. He remembered now: it was in Frodsee's room at Magdalen. There was a tall chap, with curly, dark hair sitting on Frodsee's table, swinging his legs. He was in "shorts," and his bare knees and stockings were splashed with mud. Frodsee himself was standing by the window declaiming his ridiculous jingle. And there was a third boy there who was laughing uncontrollably.

With the saintly Cybeline.

He wished he could remember the rest of the words. The sun was streaming through the window, and the young willows were whispering above the river. The jingle finished, and they all laughed, and one laugh rang out above the rest. Strange that it should all come rushing back to him at that moment—the free ring of his own laughter across the years! He had something then, he could n't think what it was— something that he had since lost.

"Even if in the end we have to sacrifice some of these minor principles, I am inclined to think, sir, that the broader issues will be better served. The interests of the party are interdependent—"

Nielson was speaking, nervously twisting the cigar in his mouth.

He made a desperate plunge to find his place in the flow of this desultory discussion. He mumbled some inchoate remark upon the land laws. It was not in any way germane to what had just been said, and he knew it; only he wanted them to draw him back among them, to protect him from the mood of perverse memories that strove to increase his melancholy.

But the memory of that laugh unnerved him. He could not concentrate. He longed once more for Dilgerson, or for some power that would give him a grip upon his concrete existence. He rose from the table, and led his guests back into the Japanese room. He lighted a cigar and, contrary to his custom, he indulged in a liqueur. His guests formed themselves into little groups, and he hovered between them, afraid to remain with either long in case they should discover his horror, that in that hour, all through a boy's laugh, he had lost the power to concentrate.

Perhaps something in his manner conveyed itself to his guests, for they broke up early, first old Griggs, then Nielson, then Brodray and the boy. He shook the boy's hand, but made no comment.

Lanyon took his departure alone, and Tippins followed. Lord Bowel seemed the only one disposed to remain. He sank back in an easy-chair and talked interminably, unaware of any psychologic change in the atmosphere of the room. He found a patient listener in Gregory Caste, to whom the discussions of a government official were as balm.

The host moved restlessly, blinking at his two remaining guests. Sometimes he would sit furtively on the edge of a chair and listen and nod his head and say: "Yes, yes; I quite agree. Yes; that is so."

Then he would rise and walk to the fireplace and move some object an inch or two from the position in which it was placed and then move it back again. He drank a glass of lemon-water, a row of which were placed on a silver tray by the Wall, and smoked another cigarette. Then the instinct of common courtesy prompted him once more to join his two remaining guests. He looked closely at Lord Bowel's heavy cheeks, and a curious feeling of disgust came over him. The voice of the board of trade official boomed on luxuriously about the arts of Eastern people, about ceramics, about the diseases of bees, the iniquity of licensing restrictions, the influence of Chaldean teaching on modern theology, on the best hotel in Paris, on the vacillating character of the principal leaders of the opposition. There seemed no end to the variety of theme, and no break in the dull monotony of voice.

It must have been well after midnight that Lord Bowel suddenly sighed heavily and rose. He took his host's hand and said gloomily:

"It has been a most delightful evening."

He watched the two men pass out into the hall, and saw Gales come ponderously forward and help them with their coats. Then he drew back and looked into the fire. He pressed his hand to his brow. He had not a headache, but he felt peculiarly exhausted, as though he had been through some great strain. In the fire he saw again the nodding heads of willows and the young clouds scudding before the wind. He started. He could not understand; he could have sworn that at that moment he again heard some one laugh. He looked round to convince himself that he was alone in the room. He shivered and stood up. He was not well. He was getting old. A time comes to all men—anyway, he had not been a failure. He had succeeded, in fact, beyond his wildest dreams. His name was known to every one in England. His features even graced the pages of the satiric journals. He was the "safe" man of the party. One paper had nicknamed him "Trumps," the safest card in the pack. It was something to have achieved this, even if he had sacrificed things, impulses, convictions, passions, the fierce joy of expressing his primitive self. Perhaps in the process he had lost something.

Ah, God! He wished the young man had not laughed.

There was a gentle tap on the door, and Gales came in.

"Oh, I beg your pardon, sir," he murmured softly.

"It's all right. I'm going to bed."

He rose weakly from the chair and went up-stairs. Once more in the bedroom, the silence tormented him. The furniture seemed no longer his own, no longer an expression of himself, but a cold, frigid statement of dead conformity. He touched the bed, and then walked up and down. What could he do? He had no power to combat the strange terrors of remorse that flooded him. He sat there silently waiting for the mood to pass. He knew that if he struggled it would pass. He would be himself again. It was all so foolish, so unworthy of him. He kept saying that to himself, but underneath it all something else seemed stirring—something that went to the roots of his being and shook him violently.

He waited there a long time till the house seemed given over to the embraces of the night, then he stealthily crept down-stairs again. It was all in darkness. He turned on the light in the hall and dining-room. He wandered to his accustomed chair at the dining-table and huddled into it. He struggled to piece together the memories of days of freedom and splendor when he had sacrificed nothing, when life was an open book.

He visualized little incidents of his childhood and school-days, but they seemed trivial and without significance or humor.

Ah, God! if he could laugh!

The Chinese Philosopher and the European War

It may seem a remarkable fact that in the World War in which nearly all nations are engaged, the oldest, wisest, and greatest nation is not only not participating, but is apparently looked upon as a negligible quantity by the belligerent powers. Surely no greater tribute could be paid to the wisdom and the greatness of the Chinese.

Some one has said that "No man was ever so wise as some Chinamen look." But will not these cataclysmal European happenings demonstrate a denial of this statement? Will they not prove that some one is as wise as some Chinamen look, and that person the Chinaman? In his rock garden near Peking the Chinese philosopher sits fanning himself. His mind communes with the spirits of his ancestors, and meditates upon the unforgetable wisdom of the Lord Confucius.

He recalls how a few idle centuries ago the continuity of these peaceful meditations was disturbed by the sudden arrival of restless infidels on his shores. Even now he can see their strained, feverish faces. To the trained eye they differed from one another; they spoke different languages, wore different clothes, had different casts of countenance, but to the all-seeing eye they were fundamentally the same. They preached the same doctrine—a doctrine they labeled "progress, civilization." They professed several mushroom faiths, the dominant one being called "Christianity," concerning which they differed profoundly, and split up into many subdivisions. The Chinese philosopher recalls the faces of their emissaries who came to him and said:

"Wake! You must advance, you must bestir yourself!" He can almost recall the tones of mild remonstrance of his own voice.

"To what end?"

"To progress. To become civilized, to enter into the great world competition."

They hardly stayed to listen to the serene philosophy which his master would have inspired him to instil into them if they had stayed to listen, they were in so restless a hurry. They said:

"If you do not do this, we will destroy you."

They were off again to struggle with one another for good positions on his shores, there to carry on their strange and unaccountable practices of buying and selling, and distributing soul-destroying spirits to the undisciplined, and to erect tin temples to their parvenu Gods. He saw their fussy gunboats on his rivers destroying human life.

Some there were who were disturbed by these actions, and came to him and said:

"What shall we do concerning this? Shall China stretch forth her hand?"

And he had answered:

"China is linked to the sun and moon by immemorial ties. Look into your heart, my children, and read the words of the All-Wise."

And then, as the centuries rolled by, he observed that it was not China they destroyed; it was one another. The wind bells tinkle under the eaves of the pagoda. Soon in all her glory the sun will be setting. A messenger enters and kneels in low obeisance.

"Excellency, the Western World is at war. Already ten million men have fallen by the sword."

"Ai-e-e!" He draws the wind through his teeth with a whistling inflection. "What Western World is this?" he asked at length.

"They who enunciate the doctrine of progress, civilization, culture, O Excellency!"

"Ai-e-e!"

He meditates upon this for some time. He harbors no feelings of animosity against these people who had threatened to destroy him; only his heart is filled with a strange, pitying misgiving that there should be so much lack of culture, so little appreciation of the value of inner progress, and so exaggerated a sense of the value of outer progress.

Wood-pigeons are cooing in their cot above the temple, and the sound, mingling with the low chanting of a priest, tends to emphasize the tranquillity of the evening. Ten million men! It is very sad, very deplorable; but he banishes these melancholy thoughts, for he knows that his mind must be occupied with far more important matters. It is the hour when, in strict accordance with immemorial precepts, he must look into his own soul.

Cricket

It is all so incredibly long ago that you must not ask me to remember the scores. In fact, even of the result I am a little dubious. I only know that it was on just such a day as this that we were all mooning round Bunty Cartwright's garden after breakfast, smoking, and watching the great bumblebees hanging heavily on the flowers. Along the flagged pathway to the house were standard rose-trees the blossoms and perfume of which excited one pleasantly. It was jolly to be in flannels and to feel the sun on one's skin, for the day promised to be hot.

I remember that for years it had been a tradition for dear old Bunty to ask us all down for the week. There were usually eight or nine of us, and we made up our team with the doctor and his son and one or two other odds and ends of chaps in the neighborhood. I know that on this day he had secured the services of Dawkin, a very fast bowler from a town near by, for Celminster, the team we were to play, were reputed to be a very hot lot.

As we stood there laughing and talking,—Bunty and Tony Peebles were sitting within the stone porch, I remember, trying to finish a game of chess started the previous evening,—there was the crunch of wheels on the road, and the brake arrived, accompanied by the doctor's son, a thin slip of a boy on a bicycle.

Then there was the usual bustle of putting up cricket-bags and going back for things one had forgotten, and the inevitable "chipping" of "Togs," a boy whose real name I have forgotten, but who was always last in everything, even in the order of going in. It must have been fully half an hour before we made a start, and then the doctor had n't arrived. However, he came up at the last minute, his jolly red face beaming and perspiring. Some of the chaps cycled, and soon left us behind, but I think we were seven on the brake. It was good to be high up and to feel the wind blowing gently on our faces from the sea. We passed villages of amazing beauty nestling in the hollows of the downs, and rumbled on our way to the accompaniment of lowing sheep and the doctor's rich, burring voice talking of cricket and the song of the lark overhead that sang in praise of this day of festival.

It was good to laugh and talk and watch the white ribbon of the road stretching far ahead, then dipping behind a stretch of woodland. It was good to feel the thrill of excited anticipation as we approached the outskirts of Celminster. What sort of ground would it be? What were their bowlers like? Who would come off for us?

It was good to see the grinning, friendly faces of the villagers and then to descend from the brake, to nod in that curiously self-conscious way we have as a race to our opponents and then to survey the field. And is there in the whole of England a more beautiful place than the Celminster cricket-ground?

On one side is a clump of buildings dominated by the straggling yards and outhouses belonging to the Bull Inn. On the farther side is a fence, and just beyond a stream bordered by young willows. At right angles to the inn is a thick cluster of elms,—a small wood, in fact,—while on the fourth side a low, gray stone wall separates the field from the road. Across the road may be seen the spire of a church, the fabric hidden by the trees, and away beyond the downs quiver in the sunlight.

In the corner of the field is a rough pavilion faced with half-timber, and a white flagstaff with the colors of the Celminster Cricket Club fluttering at its summit.

Members of the Celminster Club were practising in little knots about the field, and a crowd of small boys were sitting on a long wooden bench, shouting indescribably, and some were playing mock games with sticks and rubber balls. A few aged inhabitants looked at us with lazy interest and touched their hats.

A little man with a square chin and an auburn mustache came out and grinned at us and asked for Mr. Cartwright. We discovered that he was the local wheelwright and the Celminster captain. He showed us our room in the pavilion and called Bunty "sir." Of course Bunty lost the toss. He always did during that week, and this led to considerably more "chipping," and we turned out to field.

No one who has never experienced it can ever appreciate the tense joy of a cricketer when he comes out to begin a match. The gaiety of the morning, when the light is at its best and all one's senses are alert; the sense of being among splendid deeds that are yet unborn; and then the jolly red ball! How we love to clutch it with a sort of romantic exultation and toss it to one another! For it is upon it that the story of the day will turn. It is the scarlet symbol of our well-ordered adventure, as yet untouched and virginal, and yet strangely pregnant of unaccomplished actions. What story will it have to tell when the day is done? Who will drop catches with it? Who destroy its virgin loveliness with a fearful drive against the stone wall?

As I have stated, it happened all so long ago that I cannot clearly remember many of the details of that match, but curiously enough I remember the first over that Dawkin sent down very vividly.

A very tall man came in to bat. The first ball he played straight back to the bowler; the second was a "yorker" and just missed his wicket; the third he drove hard to mid-off, and Bunty stopped it; the fourth he stopped with his pads; the fifth he played back to the bowler again; and the sixth knocked his leg stump clean out of the ground.

One wicket for no runs! We flung the scarlet symbol backward and forward in a great state of excitement, with visions of a freak match, the whole side of our opponents being out for ten runs, and so on. I remember the glum face of their umpire, a genial corn merchant, dressed in a white coat and a bowler hat, with a bewildering number of sweaters tied round his neck, glancing apprehensively at the pavilion. I remember that the next man in was the little wheelwright, and he looked very solemn and tense. The first three balls missed his wicket by inches, then he stopped them. My recollection of the rest of that morning was a vision of the little wheelwright, with his chin thrust forward, frowning at the bowlers. He had a peculiarly uncomfortable stance at the wicket, but he played very straight. He kept Dawkin out for about five overs, then he started pulling him round to leg. The wicket was rather fiery, and Dawkin was very fast. The wheelwright was hit three times on the thigh, twice on the chest, and numberless times on the arms, and one ball got up and glanced oft his scalp; but he did not waver. He plodded on, lying in wait for the short ball to hook to leg. I do not remember how many he made, but it was a great innings. He took the heart out of Dawkin, and encouraged one or two of the others to hit with courage. He was caught at last by a brilliant catch by Arthur Booth running in from long leg.

One advantage of a village team like Celminster is that they have no "tail," or, rather, that you never know what the tail will do. You know by the costume that they have a tail, for the first four or five batsmen appear in complete outfits of white flannels and sweaters, and then the costumes start varying in a wonderful degree. Number six appears in a black waistcoat with white flannel trousers, number seven with brown pads and black boots, number eight with a blue shirt and brown trousers, and so on to the last man, who is dressed uncommonly like a verger. But this rallentando of sartorial equipment does not in any way represent the run-getting ability of the team, for suddenly some gentleman inappropriately appareled, who gives the impression of never having had a bat in his hand before, will lash out and score twenty-five runs off one over. On this particular occasion I remember one man who came in about ninth, and who wore one brown pad and sand-shoes, and had on a blue shirt with a dicky and a collar, but no tie, and who stood right in front of his wicket, looked grimly at Dawkin, and then hit him for two sixes, a four, and a five, to the roaring accompaniment of "Good old Jar-r-ge!" from the row of small boys near the pavilion. The fifth ball hit his pad and he was given out l. b. w. He gave no expression of surprise, disappointment, or disgust, but just walked grimly back to the pavilion. Celminster were all out before lunch, but I cannot let the last man—the verger—retire (he was bowled first ball off his foot) before speaking of our wicket-keeper, Jimmy Guilsworth.

Jimmy Guilsworth was in my opinion an ideal wicket-keeper. He was a little chap and wore glasses, but his figure was solid and homely. He was by profession something of a poet, and wrote lyrics in the Celtic-twilight manner. He played cricket rarely, but when he did, he was instinctively made wicket-keeper. He had that curious, sympathetic mothering quality which every good wicket-keeper should have. The first business of a wicket-keeper is to make the opposing batsmen feel at home. When the man comes in trembling and nervous, the wicket-keeper should make some reassuring remark, something that at once establishes a bond of understanding between honorable opponents. When the batsman is struck on the elbow it is the wicket-keeper who should rush up and administer first aid or spiritual comfort. And when the batsman is bowled or caught, he should say, "Hard luck, sir!"

At the same time it is his business to mother the bowlers on his own side. He must be continually encouraging them and sympathizing with them, but in a subdued voice, so that the batsman does not hear. And, moreover, he must be prepared to act as chief of staff to the captain. He must advise him on the change of bowlers and on the disposition of the field. All of this requires great tact, understanding, and perspicacity.

All these qualities Jimmy Guilsworth had in a marked degree. If he sometimes dropped catches and never stood near enough to stump any one, what was that to the sympathetic way he said, "Oh, hard luck, sir!" to an opposing batsman when he was bowled by a slow long-hop, or the convincing way he would call out, "Oh, well hit, sir!" when another opponent pulled a half-volley for four. What could have been more encouraging than the way he would rest his hand on young Booth's shoulder after he had bowled a disappointing over, and say: "I say, old chap, you're in great form. Could you pitch 'em up just a wee bit?" When things were going badly for the side, Jimmy would grin and whisper into Cartwright's ear. Then there would be a consultation and a change of bowlers, or some one would come closer up to third-man, and, lo! in no time something would happen.

But it is lunch-time. In the pavilion a long table is set with a clean cloth and napkins and with gay bowls of salad. On a side-table is a wonderful array of cold joints, hams, cold lamb, and pies. We sit down, talking of the game. Curiously enough, we do not mix with our opponents. We sit at one end, and they occupy the other, but we grin at one another, and the men sitting at the point of contact of the two parties occasionally proffer a remark.

Some girls appear to wait, and a fat man in shirt-sleeves who produces ale and ginger-beer from some mysterious corner. And what a lunch it is! Does ever veal-and-ham pie taste so good as it does in the pavilion after the morning chasing a ball? And then tarts and fruit and custard and a large yellow cheese, how splendid it all seems, with the buzz of conversation and the bright sun through the open door! Does anything lend a fuller flavor to the inevitable pipe than such a lunch, mellowed by the rough flavor of a pint of shandy-gaff?

We stroll out again into the sun and puff tranquilly, and some of us gather round old Bob Parsons, the corn merchant, and listen to his panegyric of cricket as played "in the old days." He's seen a lot of cricket in his time, old Bob. His bony, weather-beaten face wrinkles, and his clear, ingenuous eyes blink at the heavens as he recalls famous men: "Johnny Strutt he was a good 'un. Aye, and ye should ha' seen old Tom Kennett bowl in his time. Nine wicket' he took agenst Kailhurst, hittin' the wood every toime. Fast he were, faster 'n they bowl now. Fower bahls he bahl fast, then put up a slow."

He shakes his head meditatively, as though the contemplation of the diabolical cunning of bowling a slow ball after four fast ones was almost too much to believe, as though it was a demonstration of intellectual calisthenics that this generation could not appreciate.

It is now the turn of our opponents to take the field, while we eagerly scan the score-sheet to see the order of going in, and restlessly move about the pavilion, trying on pads and making efforts not to appear nervous.

And with what a tense emotion we watch our first two men open the innings! It is with a gasp of relief we see Jimmy Guilsworth cut a fast ball for two, and know, at any rate, we have made a more fortunate start than our opponents did.

I do not remember how many runs we made that afternoon, though as we were out about tea-time, I believe we just passed the Celminster total, but I remember that to our joy Bunty Cartwright came off. He had been unlucky all the week, but this was his joy-day. He seemed cheerful and confident when he went in, and he was let off on the boundary off the first ball! After that he did not make a mistake.

It was a joy to watch Bunty bat. He was tall and graceful, and he sprang to meet the ball like a wave scudding against a rock. He seemed to epitomize the dancing sunlight, a thing of joy expressing the fullness of the crowded hour. His hair blew over his face, and one could catch the gleam of satisfaction that radiated from him as he panted on his bat after running out a five.

He was not a great cricketer, none of us was, but he had a good eye, the heart of a lion, and he loved the game.

I believe I made eight or nine. I know I made a cut for four. The recollection of it IS very keen to this day, and the satisfying joy of seeing the ball scudding along the ground a yard out of the reach of point. It made me very happy. And then one of those balls came along that one knows nothing about. How remarkable it is that a bowler who appears so harmless from the pavilion seems terrifying and demoniacal when he comes tearing down the crease toward you!

Yes, I'm sure we passed the Celminster total now, for I remember at tea-time discussing the possibilities of winning by a single innings if we got Celminster out for forty.

After tea, for some reason or other, one smokes cigarettes. We strolled into a yard at the back of the Bull Inn, and there was a wicket gate leading to a lawn where some wonderful old men whose language was almost incomprehensible were drinking ale and playing bowls. At the side were some tall sunflowers growing amid piles of manure.

Some one in the pavilion rang a bell, and we languidly returned to take the field once more.

I remember that it was late in the afternoon that a strange thing happened to me. I was fielding out in the long field not thirty yards from the stream. Tony Peebles was bowling from the end where I was fielding. I noted his ambling run up to the wicket and the graceful action of his arm as he swung the ball across. A little incident happened, a thing trivial at the time, but which one afterward remembers. The batsman hit a ball rather low on the off side, which the doctor's son caught or stopped on the ground. There was an appeal for a catch, given in the batsman's favor; but for some reason or other he thought the umpire had said "out," and he started walking to the pavilion. He was at least two yards out of his crease when the doctor's son threw the ball to Jimmy Guilsworth at the wicket. Jimmy had the wicket at his mercy, but instead of putting it down he threw it back to the bowler. It was perhaps a trivial thing, but it epitomized the game we played. One does not take advantage of a mistake. It is n't done.

The sun was already beginning to Hood the valley with the excess of amber light which usually betokens his parting embrace. The stretch of level grass became alive and vibrant, tremblingly golden against the long, crisp shadows cast from the elms. The elms themselves nodded contentedly, and down by the stream flickered little white patches of children's frocks. Everything suddenly seemed to become more vivid and transcendent. As if aware of the splendor of that moment, all the little things struggled to express themselves more actively. The birds and little insects in solemn unison praised God, or, rather, to my mind, at that moment they praised England, the land that gave them such a glorious setting. The white-clad figures on the sunlit field, the smoke from the old buildings by the inn trailing lazily sk3'ward, the comfortable buzz of the voices of some villagers lying on their stomachs on the grass—ah, my dear land!

I don't know how it was, but at that moment I felt a curious contraction of the heart, like one who looks into the face of a lover who is going on a journey. Perhaps a townsman gets a little tired at the end of a day in the field, or the feeling may have been due to the Cassandra-like dirge of a flock of rooks that swung across the sky and settled in the elms.

The bat, cut from a willow down by the stream; the stumps; the leather ball; the symbol of the wicket, the level lawn cut and rolled and true—all these things were redolent of the land we moved on. They spoke of the love of trees and wind and sun and the equipoise of man in nature's setting. They symbolized our race, slow-moving and serene, with a certain sensuous joy in movement, a love of straightness, and an indestructible faith in custom. Ah, that the beauty of that hour should fade, that the splendor and serenity of it all should pass away! Strange waves of misgiving flooded me.

If it should be all too slow-moving, too serene! If at that moment the wheels of the Juggernaut of evolution were already on their way to crush the splendor of it beneath their weight!

Ah, my dear land, if you should be in danger! If one day another match should come in which you would measure yourself against—some unknown terrors! I was aware at that moment of a poignant sense of prayer that when your trial should come it would find you worthy of the clean sanity of that sunlit field; and if in the end you should go down, as everything in nature does go down before the scythe of Time, the rooks up there in the elms should cry aloud your epitaph. They are very old and wise, these rooks; they watched the last of the Ptolemys pass from Egypt, they moaned above Carthage and Troy, and warned the Roman pretors of the coming of Attila. And the epitaph they shall make for you—for they saw the little incident of Jimmy Guilsworth and the doctor's son—shall be, "Whatever you may say of these English, they played the game."

I think those small boys down by the pavilion made too much fuss about the catch I muffed. Of course I did get both hands to it, and as a matter of fact the sun was not in my eyes; but I think I started a bit late, and it seemed to be screwing horribly. Ironical jeers are not comforting. Bunty, like the dear good sportsman he is, merely called out:

"Dreaming there?"

But it was a wretched moment. I remember slinking across at the over, feeling like an animal that has contracted a disease and is ashamed to be seen, and my mental condition was by no means improved by the cheap sarcasms of young Booth or Eric Ganton. We did not get Celminster out for the second time, and the certainty that the result would not be affected by the second innings led to introduction of strange and unlikely bowlers being put on and given their chance. I remember that just at the end of the day even young "Togs" was tired. He sent down three most extraordinary balls that went nowhere within reach of the batsman, the fourth was a full pitch, and a young rustic giant who was then batting promptly hit it right over the pavilion. The next ball was very short and came on the leg side. I was fielding at short leg, and I saw the batsman hunching his shoulders for a fearful swipe. I felt in a horrible funk. I heard the loud crack of the ball on the willow, and I was aware of it coming straight at my head. I fell back in an ineffectual sort of manner, and despairingly threw up my hands in a sort of self-defense. And then an amazing thing happened: the ball went bang into my left hand and stopped there. I slipped and fell, but somehow I managed to hang on to the ball. I remember hearing a loud shout, and suddenly the pain of impact vanished in the realization that I had brought oft a hot catch. It was a golden moment. The match was over. I remember all our chaps shouting and laughing, and young "Togs" rushing up and throwing his arms round me in a mock embrace. We ambled back to the pavilion, and it suddenly struck me how good-looking most of our men were, even Tony Peebles, whom I had always looked upon as the plainest of the plain. My heart warmed toward Bunty with a passionate zeal when he struck me on the back and said: "Good man! You 've more than retrieved your muff in the long field."

I know they ragged me frightfully in the pavilion when we were changing, but it was no effort to take it good-humoredly. I felt ridiculously proud.

We took a long time getting away, there was so much rubbing down and talking to be done, and then there was the difficulty of getting Len Booth out of the Bull Inn. He had a romantic passion for drinking ale with the yokels, and a boy had stuck a pin into one of Ganton's tires, and he had to find a bicycle shop and get it mended. It was getting dark when we all got established once more in the brake.

I remember vividly turning the corner in the High Street and looking back on the solemn profile of the inn. The sky was almost colorless, just a glow of warmth, and already in some of the windows lamps were appearing. We huddled together contentedly in the brake, and I saw the firm lines of Bunty's face as he leaned over a match, lighting his pipe.

The grass is long to-day in the field where we played Celminster, and down by the stream are two square, unattractive buildings, covered with zinc roofing, where is heard the dull roar of machinery. The ravages of time cannot eradicate from my memory the vision of Bunty's face leaning over his pipe or the pleasant buzz of the village voices as we clattered among them in the High Street or the sight of the old corn merchant's face as he came up and spoke to Bunty (Bunty had stopped the brake to get more tobacco) and touched his hat and said:

"Good noight, sir. Good luck to 'ee!"

Decades have passed, and I have to press the spring of my memory to bring these things back; but when they come they are very dear to me.

I know that in the wind that blows above Gallipoli you will find the whispers of the great faith that Bunty died for. Eric Ganton, young Booth, and Jimmy Guilsworth, where are they? In vain the soil of Flanders strives to clog the free spirit of my friends.

"Good noight, sir. Good luck to 'ee!"

Again I see the old man's face as I gaze across the field where the long grass grows, and I see the red ball tossed hither and thither, with its story still unfinished, and I hear the sound of Jimmy's voice:

"Oh, well hit, sir!" as he encourages an opponent.

The times have changed since then, but you cannot destroy these things. Manners have changed, customs have changed, even the faces of men have changed; and yet this calendar on my knee is trying to tell me that it all happened two years ago to-day!

And overhead the garrulous rooks seem strangely flustered.

Mrs. Huggins's Hun

Mrs. Huggins's manifestation of antipathy to her prospective son-in-law was a thing to be seen to be believed. She bridled at the sight of him. She lashed him with her tongue on every conceivable occasion. She snubbed, derided, buffeted him. She could find no virtue in his appearance, manners, or character. She hated him with consuming wrath, and did not hesitate to flaunt her animadversion in his face or in the face of her friends or of her daughter Maggie. Maggie was Mrs. Muggins's only child, and Mrs. Huggins was a widow running a boarding-house in Camden Town. Maggie was her ewe-lamb, the light of her existence, whose simple, unsophisticated character had been suddenly, within two months, entirely demoralized by the advent of this meteoric youth. Quentin Livermore had appeared from the blue, when Mrs. Huggins was very distracted at her unlet rooms, and had applied for her first floor, for which he offered a good price. He was a weak-faced, flashy, old-young man, anything between thirty and forty. He dressed gorgeously, lived sumptuously, and was employed in some government department. He was in the house less than twenty-four hours when he began to make love to Maggie, and it was the change in Maggie which particularly annoyed Mrs. Huggins. Maggie was a stenographer in a local store, earning good money, and a simple, natural girl; but when Mr. Livermore appeared on the scene, she began to speak with an affected lisp, to wear fal-lals and gew-gaws, and to do her hair in strange bangs and buns. In a few days they were going out for strolls together after supper. In a fortnight he was taking her to theaters and cinemas. In six weeks they were to all intents and purposes engaged. At least, they said they were engaged. Mrs. Huggins said they were not. In fact, she told her friend Mrs. O'Neil, in-the private bar of the Staff of Life, that she would "see that slobberin' shark damned" before he should go off with her Mag.

But on the morning when this story begins Mrs. Huggins was in a very perturbed state. It was a pleasant June morning, and she had finished her housework. She sat down to enjoy a well-merited glass of stout and to review the situation. Maggie had gone away for a few days' holiday, to stay with some cousins in Essex, and the evening before she had left there had been a terrible rumpus. Maggie had come home with her hair bobbed, looking like some wretched office-boy. After Mrs, Huggins had vented her opinion upon this contemptible metamorphosis and had cried a little, she went out, and, returning late in the evening, found her Maggie lolling on a couch in Mr. Livermore's room, smoking cigarettes and drinking port wine! It was a climax in every sense, and to add to her misfortune the Bean family, who occupied the third and a part of the fourth floor, suddenly left to go and live at Mendon, near the aëroplane works, where they were nearly all employed.

Mrs. Huggins had now no lodgers except the insufferable Mr. Livermore. It would be impossible to keep up her refined establishment on the twenty-five shillings a week that Livermore paid her without breaking into her hard-earned savings. But this fact did not disturb Mrs. Huggins so much as the difficulty of furthering a more ambitious project, which was nothing less than to get rid of Mr. Livermore while Maggie was away.

Mrs. Huggins blew the froth off the stout, took a long draft, wiped her mouth on her apron, and then continued to ponder upon the problem. No light came to her, and she was about to repeat the operation when she was disturbed by the clatter of a four-wheeled cab driving up to the front door. She looked up through the kitchen window and beheld a strange sight. The cab was laden with a most peculiar collection of trunks and boxes, and, standing by the front doorstep, was a fat man holding a cage with a canary in one hand and a violin-case in the other.

"Ah, a new lodger at last!" thought Mrs. Huggins, and she slipped off her apron and hurried up-stairs. When she opened the front door, she noticed that the fat man had thick spectacles, a Homburg hat much too small for his head, and a tuft of yellow beard between two of his innumerable chins. He put down the canary and removed his hat.

"Have I the honor to speak to the honored Mrs. Huggins?" he said.

"Mrs. Huggins is my name," answered that lady.

"Ah, so? May I a word with you?" He walked deliberately into the hall and once more set down the canary and the violin. He then produced a sheaf of papers.

"I have been regommended. May I have the pleasure of your hospitality for some time?"

"I have some rooms to let," replied Mrs. Huggins, evasively.

He bowed, and blew his nose.

"I must eggsplain in ze first place, goot lady, I am a Sherman."

There was a perceptible pause while the two eyed each other; then Mrs. Huggins said explosively:

"Oh, I can't take no dirty 'Uns in my 'ouse."

It might perhaps be mentioned at this point that the speech of Mrs. Huggins was always characterized by directness and force. The Hun bowed once more and replied:

"The matter is already at your disposition, good lady. I state my case. If you gan gonsider it, I gan assure you that all my papers are in order. The London poliss officers know me. I report to zem. I have my passports, my permits. Everything in order. I pay you vell."

Mrs. Huggins blinked at the German and blinked at the cab. The cab looked somewhat imposing, with its large trunks, and the German's face was eminently homely and kind. Her eye wandered from it to the canary, and then along the wall to the hall stand, and came to a stop at Livermore's felt hat. She equivocated.

"What sort of rooms do you want?" she said.

At this compromise of tone the Hun assumed the arbitrariness of his race. He put his things down on the hall chairs and became voluble and convincing. He was a watch- and clock-maker. His business in Hackney had been destroyed by fire. He had been offered an excellent position at a colleague's in Camden Town, the said colleague being sick and in urgent need of help. He was simple in his requirements; a bed, a breakfast, occasionally a supper. His name was Schmidt, Karl Schmidt. He was willing to pay three pounds a week for the rooms, payment in advance. He had endless "regommendations." Mrs. Huggins found herself following him up and down stairs, helping him in with trunks, and listening abstractedly. In a vague way she took to the Hun, and her mind was active with a scheme to use him for her own ends. All the trunks were installed in the third-floor rooms, and she observed him take out an old string purse and say to the cabman:

"Now have we all the paggages installed. So."

He paid the cabman, came into the hall, and shut the door. He walked ponderously up-stairs, humming to himself. Mrs. Huggins heard him busy with bunches of keys, opening and shutting trunks and putting things away in drawers. The whole thing had happened so suddenly that Mrs. Huggins still could not decide her course of action. She went down-stairs and put some potatoes on to boil. After a time she heard the Hun coming heavily down to the hall again. She went up to meet him. He waved three one-pound treasury-notes in the air and placed them on the hall-table.

"Mrs. Huggins," he said, "please to be goot enough to allow me to present you with zese. I shall be very gomfortable here. It is all satisfactory. I go now to my colleague in pizness. Then I go to eggsplain to the poliss. It is all in order. Yes. I shall not be returnable since zis evening, perhaps eight o'gloch, perhaps nine o'gloch. In any vay, I gom back before ten o'gloch. Oh, yes, before ten o'gloch." He laughed boisterously, bowed, and went out. Mrs. Huggins stared at the door, then went to the window and watched him cross the street.

"Well, I'm demned!" she muttered to herself, and fingered the three crisp treasury-notes in her hand. She went up to his room and touched all his trunks and small effects. Most of his things were locked up. She said, "Cheep! cheep!" to the canary three times, and then went down-stairs and had her dinner.

And that afternoon Mrs. Huggins became very busy. In apron, and with bare arms and a broom, she worked as she had not worked for months. The details may be spared, but the principal effect must be observed that by six-thirty that evening all Herr Fritz's luggage and effects had been installed in the first-floor room, and all Mr. Quentin Livermore's property had been piled up in a heap in the hall!

We shall also take the liberty of passing over the details of the interview which took place between Mrs. Huggins and Mr. Livermore when he came in at seven o'clock that evening on his way to change his clothes and go down West to dine. It need only be said that the accumulated antipathy of their two months' intercourse reached a climax. There may have been faults on both sides, but Mrs. Huggins was in one of her most masterful moods, and she was, moreover, armed with a brush. Mr. Livermore had only a cane and his superciliousness. He was, indeed, rather frightened, and his sneering comments on her personal appearance had little sting. His ultimate decision to leave at once and go over to Mrs. Hayward's, so that he would still be where Maggie would find him, and where, in any case, it was tolerably clean, and the landlady knew how to cook, was the only shaft which told at all, for Mrs. Hayward and Mrs. Huggins were notorious rivals. In the end a cab was secured, and by eight o'clock the triumphant Mrs. Huggins had slammed the door on her hated lodger, with a final threat that "if she saw 'im going about with 'er gal she'd bang 'im over the chops with a broom."

So excited and exhilarated was Mrs. Huggins by her victory that when he had gone, she felt it incumbent upon her to dash down to the Staff of Life for ten minutes to get a glass of beer and to unburden herself to Mrs. O'Neil. Not finding her friend there, she had two glasses of beer and hurried back. On arriving at the corner of her street she had another surprise. A taxi was standing outside her door, and a short gentleman with a dark mustache and pointed beard was banging on her door and looking up at the windows.

"Gawd's truth! What is it now?" muttered Mrs. Huggins, hurrying up.

On approaching the stranger, he turned and looked at her.

"Well, what is it?" she asked.

The gentleman smiled very charmingly and made an elaborate bow.

"Ah," he exclaimed, "so at last I have the pleasure of addressing the charming Madame Huggins! Madame, my compliments. May I address you on a professional mattare?"

He slipped a visiting-card into her hand on which was printed, "M. Jules de la Roche, 29B rue Dormi, Paris."

Mrs. Huggins stared at the card and opened her front door.

"O my Gawd!" was all that occurred to her to remark. The Frenchman—for so he apparently was— bowed again, and followed her into the hall.

"You must pardon my precipitate manners," he said. "I am very pressed. I am in London on business connnected with the French Red Cross. I have a peculiar dislike to hotels, and a lady I met in the train was kind enough to refer me to your charming pension. I shall owe you a thousand thanks if you will be kind enough to allow me to enjoy your hospitality if only for a few days, or perhaps weeks. Whatever you can do—" He waved his arms and looked quickly, almost beseechingly, round the little hall.

Mrs. Huggins wiped her mouth on her apron, and stared at the Frenchman.

"Well, this is a rum go!" she remarked I at last. "I 've got a German on the first floor, a nice, quiet feller. And now you 're a Frenchy! Now, look here; if I take you in, I'm not goin' to 'ave any fightin' goin' on. D' you understand that?"

The Frenchman gave her one of his quick glances and laughed.

"My dear madame," he exclaimed, "what ees eet to me? I am of entirely a gentle disposition, and if your friend is of gentle disposition, vy should we quarrel?"

"'E's no friend of mine," interjected Mrs. Huggins. "'E's a 'Un, but 'e's a lodger. I don't make friends of my lodgers, but I treats 'em fair. If I do the fair and square thing by them, I expect 'em to do the fair and square by me; but I won't 'ave the place turned into a bear-garden by a lot of foreigners."

M. de la Roche threw back his head and laughed.

"An admirable sentiment, chère madame. Then it is settled. I take my effects immediately to—vich floor did you mention?"

"I did n't mention no floor," replied Mrs. Huggins, "but if you like to leave it at that, I dessay I can fix you up on the third, and the terms will be three pounds a week."

The face of Mrs. Huggins was perfectly straight when she demanded this extortionate sum, neither did it show any evidence of surprise when the Frenchman quite avidly agreed, and immediately paid her three pounds down in advance. He seemed a gay and companionable gentleman. He had only one valise, which he ran up-stairs with. He paid the cabman a sum which seemed to leave that gentleman so speechless he could not even express his thanks. He chatted to Mrs. Huggins merrily about the weather, the war, the food problems, the difficulties of running a lodging-house. He was intensely sympathetic about various minor ailments of which Mrs. Huggins was a victim. He listened attentively to the history of various former lodgers, but beyond eliciting the fact that the German occupied the first floor, he showed no particular interest in his fellow-lodger. He explained that he had considerable correspondence to attend to that evening, so he did not purpose to go out; but if Mrs. Huggins could scramble him a couple of eggs on toast and make him a cup of tea, he would be eternally grateful.

Mrs. Huggins was a good cook. It was a matter she took a keen personal delight in. She would neglect her housework in order to produce some savory trifle for a pet lodger. On this occasion she surprised M. de la Roche by serving him with a large ham omelet and an apple tart.

"After yer long journey, you 'll want a bite of somethin'," she explained.

Any apprehensions she entertained that her house was to be turned into a beer-garden by a lot of quarrelsome foreigners were early dissipated. At half-past nine that evening Herr Schmidt came in and went up to his room. Ten minutes later M. Jules de la Roche, coming down-stairs, beheld the canary in its cage on a chair outside Herr Fritz's door.

"Ah, le petit bossu!" he remarked.

The door was ajar, and Herr Fritz stepped out.

"Bonsoir, monsieur," he said in his deep-chested voice. "Are you interested in canaries?"

The Frenchman bowed a friendly manner.

"My sympathies always go out to the caged, monsieur," he replied. "But what a pretty fellow! Am I right in suggesting that he is of the Belgian species?"

"No, sir," said the German. "Although they vas somet'ing similiar, zis is ze Scottish."

"Pardon," replied the Frenchman. "I ought to have known. I have lived at Terceira, in the Azores, where one hears canaries singing in the open all day. Eet ees entrancing."

"Gom inzide," said Herr Schmidt and sighed, "and let us talk. I am lonely."

Mrs. Huggins overheard this conversation from the hall beneath, and she smiled contentedly. It was a triumph, a bolt from the blue. She had ousted the wretched Livermore, and like manna from heaven these two gentle, simple foreigners, who were willing to pay through the neck, had dropped right into her lap. Her conscience mildly smote her that she had demanded so much from Herr Schmidt, but a rapid mental calculation had decided that he must pay at least double as a penalty for being a Hun, but at the same time it would n't be fair to him to take another lodger for less. She had been, in any case, prepared to bargain, and to reduce considerably her terms, and had been quite nonplussed at not being called upon to do so. So far, so good; but the difficulty of detaching the wretched Livermore from her Maggie still remained to be accomplished, for Maggie was to return the day after to-morrow, and Livermore would be sure to be always hanging about the street.

In the meantime the conversation between the two foreigners up-stairs never flagged. They became extremely friendly. The violin case laid the foundation for an intimate chat on technic, personality. Bach, nationality. From these easily devolved discussions on politics, religion, and hence, inevitably, "this regrettable war." Each man was patently sensitive of the other's feelings. They talked of everything in the abstract, and avoided as far as possible the personal equation. They found each other extremely interesting, but there arrived a point when each was aware that the other was fencing. Herr Schmidt produced a bottle of whisky and a syphon of soda, but he could not persuade M. de la Roche to partake of more than one glass. It was nearly twelve o'clock when the Frenchman suddenly said:

"Well, my dear Herr Schmidt, I have had a most entrancing evening. I suggest that you dine vif me to-morrow evening. I have made de happy discovery dat our good Mrs. Huggins is a most excellent chef. Why should ve two lonely bachelors not share our meal?"

"I gannot gonzidder anyt'ing more delightful," replied Herr Schmidt. "Only I insist that you dine vif me in my room. I glaim preeminence as ze first-floor lodger." He laughed boisterously, and after further mildly disputing the matter, it was arranged accordingly.

The dinner which Herr Schmidt prevailed upon Mrs. Huggins to supply the following evening in honor of his friend M. de la Roche was of such a nature that not only had the like never been served in Mrs. Huggins's household, but probably never before in the whole environment of Camden Town. In the first place, there were oysters and grape-fruit, soup, a baked bream, a roast fowl and several vegetables; a lemon-curd tart, Welsh rarebit, and grapes, the whole mellowed with the exhilarating complement of Italian vermuth, sparkling Moselle, and a very old brandy, to say nothing of coffee, cigars, and the dazzling conversation of the two gentlemen.

The preparation of these alluring delicacies occupied Mrs. Huggins nearly the whole of the day—a day which was marred only by a regrettable scuffle in the early morning. It happened at about half-past eight. Mrs. Huggins was at work in the kitchen when she heard a commotion going on up in the hall. Hurrying up-stairs, she found M. de la Roche arguing with Quentin Livermore. The Frenchman turned to her.

"Who is dis man, madam? I know him not. He comes into the house unbidden."

And Livermore cut in:

"I 've come to collect my letters. You 're not going to keep my letters from me."

Mrs. Huggins seized her broom and cried out:

"You get out, you dirty thief and blackmailer!"

She experienced no difficulty in routing Mr. Livermore and sending him flying up the street, and after his departure she told the whole story to M. de la Roche, who kept on repeating:

"Nom de Dieu! how shocking! Quel perfide! What a villain!" He was almost in tears.

The rest of the day passed quietly. Both the gentlemen went out soon after breakfast. Herr Schmidt did not return till seven-thirty in the evening, in time for the dinner. M. de la Roche came in at five o'clock, and persuaded Mrs. Huggins to go to the nearest haberdasher's and obtain two clean shirts for him, as, owing to his imperfect knowledge of the English tongue, he was unable to obtain the sort he required. She returned in half an hour, and M. de la Roche thanked her profusely. At eight o'clock precisely he presented himself in Herr Schmidt's room, wearing an ill-fitting evening dress peculiar to Frenchmen. Herr Schmidt was also in evening dress of an ill-fitting kind peculiar to Germans. They bowed, and shook hands cordially.

"I am indeed fortunate," remarked Herr Schmidt, "in a city so desolate as London, and in a quarter so traurig as zis, to find zo sympathetic and charming a fellow-lodger."

"Tout au contraire," replied the Frenchman. "The good fortune is exclusively to me. Ah, this London! was there ever a city so abaissé, so triste?"

"Never, never," retorted Herr Schmidt.

"Now, let me offer you a glass of goot vermuth, and then ve vill these excellent oysters circumscribe while ze goot Frau Huggins prepares ze soup."

The two men sat down, and toasted each other solemnly.

"Doubtless you haf gonsiderably traveled, frient?" remarked Herr Schmidt as he disposed of his second dozen oysters.

"I would not venture to address myself as a traveler," replied M. de la Roche. "True, I have lived in the Azores, and I am at home in Egypt, Morocco, Spain, France, and Italy. But a traveler, parbleu! it means something more than that. And you, Herr Schmidt, have you adventured far?"

"No; ze fatherland—pardon me speaking of ze fatherland in zese delicate times—ze fatherland has occupied me for most a long vile, and zen zis dear Engeland, vich I love almost as much as, it occupies me too already. For ze rest, a little Dutchman, a little Svede, a little of the sea; I am a citizen of ze vide, vide vorld, is n't it?"

"Ees eet not curious," remarked M. de la Roche as Mrs. Huggins brought in the soup; "eet appears mostly that you visit countries I have not visit, and I visit countries you not visit. Strange!"

"So it happens most nearly alvays. Now I vish much to go to America. And you?"

"Ah, America! Yes, most interesting."

"You do not go to America?"

The German looked at the Frenchman with his mild eyes, and M. de la Roche shook his head.

"No, no; I don't like." he rejoined. "It does not call to me. Interesting, yes, trèsé intéressunt; but to me too matériel. Life to me must be romance. Romance first, romance second, romance all de time."

"Efen in Camden Town?" queried Herr Schmidt, slicing the bream down the center. Then he laughed. "Well, after all, vy not? It is to be found, your romance, even in material zings. I lofe material zings, and I find zem romantic. It is a figure of ze mind. Allow me to offer you zome of zis sparkling vine, if it does not to trink a German vine you disgust."

"I am a Cat'olic," replied M. de la Roche, "bot' in my religion and in appreciation of goot t'ings. To your goot healt', Herr Schmidt, and happy days ven peace shall come."

"Happy days!" solemnly replied the German. "May the vorld vonce more to reason gom!"

The wine flowed freely. The fowl was done to a nicety. The conversation never flagged. Mrs. Huggins enjoyed the dinner almost as much as her two lodgers. They were the softest things she had ever encountered in her professional career. Visions of a bounteous time despite the war floated before her mind's eye. She even decided that she would treat them fairly and squarely. She would not take advantage of their innocence; but there would be a steady accumulation of "things left over," which were her natural perquisites. She was indeed surveying the remnants of the very solid fowl, as it reclined on a dish in the hall, and was mentally performing the skilful operation of "trimming it up" without altering the general effect of the mass, when she heard Herr Schmidt's door open and shut, and he came down the stairs quietly. In the hall he produced a large timepiece from his waistcoat-pocket, and resting one hand commandingly on her shoulder, he said:

"Mrs. Huggins, in seven minutes precisely two shentlemens vill gall to visit me. Ask no questions. Show them straight up to my room, open ze door, and say, 'Mr. Skinner and Mr. Trout.' Then close ze door and retire till I gall you vonce more again."

He gave her no opportunity to reply to these instructions, but returned to his room. As the door opened she heard him crying out:

"Pardon me, dear Monsieur de la Roche. You must try von of my Contadinos. I gan really regommend them. I brought zem myself from Amsterdam the year pefore zis distressful var."

"A thousand t'anks, my dear Herr Schmidt. It is a luxury I seldom allow myself dese days."

The gentle flow of these suave pleasantries reached their appointed crisis. Each man lay back in an easy-chair, with the divine Contadino between his teeth. On the table stood the little glasses filled with the old brandy.

"Life may be very pleasant and grassifying in the midst of vickedness and sin," murmured Herr Schmidt.

"C'est très vrai," replied M. de la Roche. "It does not do even to t'ink of dese t'ings all de time."

"Friendship is vat I value beyond all else, M. de la Roche, to your goot healt'!"

As each man raised the little glass, the door opened, and Mrs. Huggins announced:

"Mr. Trinner and Mr. Snout."

Two stolid-looking gentlemen entered, and Mrs. Huggins retired.

Herr Schmidt removed the cigar from his mouth and said:

"Good evening, gentlemen," and then without changing his position, and in a voice without any trace of German accent, he addressed M. de la Roche as follows:

"Ephraim Hyems, I have the honor to arrest you on an extraordinary warrant issued by the United States Government for embezzlement in connection with the Pennsylvania Small Arms Trust, and moreover with an attempt to convey certain information to an enemy agent in this country, under Article 36 of the Defense of the Realm Act."

The Frenchman leaned forward, and clutching the arms of the chair, he gave vent to a very un-Frenchified expression. He said:

"Gee-whiz!"

"It hardly required that native vernacular to convince me that you were not a Frenchman. As a matter of fact, I have lived for many years in Paris, and if I may say so without giving offense, Monsieur de la Roche, your French never convinced me at all."

The pseudo-Frenchman sat here apparently dazed. At length he said:

"Professionally speaking, Herr Schmidt, it is regrettable that our rôles were not reversed. It is true that I know little French, but I happen to have spent some years in Germany. I studied medicine at Leipsic. Your German is appalling. It would not deceive a London policeman. In this present case I am fully prepared to throw up my arms and to cry 'Kamerad!' only I would ask you, as a last request, whether you or your assistants would kindly extract my pocket-book from my breast-pocket, and examine my card and any other papers you or they may find. And, finally, whether you will allow me to finish this glass of very excellent brandy."

Herr Schmidt bowed.

"Trout," he said, "turn out all his pockets and hand me his pocket-book. In the meantime the gentleman can enjoy his last plunge of dissipation."

The solemn-looking sub-inspector did as he was told, and handed Herr Schmidt the pocket-book. That gentleman turned it over slowly and drew out a card. When his eyes alighted on it, his face expressed sudden amazement, and then he threw back his head and laughed explosively.

"Cyrus G. Vines!" he exclaimed. "Cyrus G. Vines of the New York police! It's quite true we 've been expecting Mr. Cyrus G. Vines for some time on this Hyems case. Holy Christopher! and are you really Cyrus G. Vines? Well, I'm damned! Also, I'm glad, if it's true. We shall require a little more evidence on that count. But in the meantime will you kindly explain your presence in Mrs. Huggins's house in Camden Town?"

Mr. Vines grinned. There was no longer any of the Frenchman about him. In fact, he carefully removed the little tuft of beard and mustache of the conventional stage Gaul. He puffed at his cigar and said:

"Unless my calculations are at fault, you will be Inspector Hartrigg. It is quite true my duty was to report right away to Scotland Yard. But it happens I'm a young man. Inspector, and I have ambitions to make good. I arrived at Liverpool last Friday; the boat was thirty hours ahead of time. I just thought I'd buzz around for a day or two on my own and see whether I could n't get the case a bit straighter to hand over. I got wise that this Hyems galoot was boarding on the first floor of this shanty. I tracked him here and found him disguised as a Hun! Do you take me?"

The "Hun" pulled at the little tuft of beard between his chins, and twirled his genuine mustache.

"Well, this is a nice go!" he said. "Between us we have missed the quarry. I confess I only traced him to this house. I did n't know which floor. But when I discovered that there was only one other lodger, and he a Frenchman, the case seemed obvious."

"Say, Inspector," interjected the American, "what was your idea of this German stunt?"

"Hyems has been further suspected of dealing with a German agent, as I have told you. I thought a nice friendly German might draw him out. That is all. It is quite true I don't know German well, although I spent a long time in France. Now, tell me what was your idea of the French stunt, Vines?"

"A Frenchman enjoys certain prerogatives," Vines smilingly replied. "He can be talkative, inquiring, sympathetic. He can even make inquiries concerning 'things of the heart' without giving offense. Now, Mrs. Huggins is a very charming and sympathetic woman, and she has a daughter, I believe, although I 've never had the pleasure of meeting her."

"That's true. But how does this affect Hyems?"

The "Frenchman" rose and said:

"Inspector, I understand that I am technically under arrest. But you have already granted me two favors while in that condition, and I am bold enough to appeal for a third. It is that you all three should accompany me to my room on the third floor and observe the devastating effect of love."

The four men trooped up-stairs, and Vines threw open the door of his bedroom. On his bed lay Mr. Livermore, neatly gagged and bound.

"This is our friend Hyems," remarked Vines. "We will remove the gag. I put it there because I did n't want our dinner disturbed by any fuss or excitement."

He removed the gag and said:

"How are you, Hyems?"

The wild-eyed man on the bed was in a state of collapse. He glanced at the other four men and closed his eyes, muttering:

"Go on. It's a do."

Inspector Hartrigg looked at the man carefully. Then he said:

"My God! you 're right. That's Hyems. Skinner and Trout, stay with this man for a few minutes. He's under arrest, remember, I 'll call you in a few minutes. Vines, come down to my room again. There are one or two points I'd like to clear up."

"Herr Schmidt" and "M. de la Roche" returned to the room below and surveyed the scene of their repast, and then both laughed.

"Come, a little more of this excellent brandy. Monsieur de la Roche, and then tell me how you accomplished your capture."

They filled their glasses once more.

"It all came fairly easy," explained Vines, "when I had once ingratiated myself with Mrs. Huggins. She's a daisy, that woman. She was full of this story about Livermore and her Maggie; but it was not till this morning, when the mail came, that I got wise on the real trend of things. Wherever I am, I always like to be right there when the mail's delivered. There's information of all sorts to be picked up even from the outside. This morning there was a long envelop franked and sealed, addressed to 'Herr Schmidt.' I was just crazy to open that communication, and I was just on the point of securing it when Mrs. Huggins came fussing into the hall. I retired to my room again for about fifteen minutes. When I got back to the hall the long envelop addressed to you had vanished, and a stranger was fingering the mail. I called for Mrs. Huggins. When she came, she soon put the stranger to flight with a broom and her tongue. I was a very sympathetic Frenchman, and then it was she told me the whole story of Mr. Livermore and her Maggie. While she was speaking, the whole truth came to me in a flash. I realized that Livermore was Hyems, but I was darned if I could place you. The capture was dead easy. In the hurried removal of Livermore's things last night, our good landlady had overlooked one or two trifles. She had apparently dumped some on that old chest at the top of the kitchen stairs. I found there a small box in which I discovered several notes and billets doux signed by 'M.' I am no mug at faking caligraphy. That afternoon I despatched a note to Mr. Livermore in the handwriting of M.

'Do come at five-thirty. Mother will be out. Tremendously important. M.'

I underlined 'tremendously important' four times. It was one of the lady's minor characteristics. At five-thirty Mrs. Huggins was very considerately buying me a couple of shirts in the High Street. I was alone in the house. I let Mr. Livermore in. The rest was just dead easy—as easy as skinning a rabbit.'

"Herr Fritz" laughed.

"Well, Vines," he said, "I congratulate you. It was a smart piece of work. I feel convinced you are destined to 'make good.' It looks as though our friend would even now be free if he had n't been so enterprising as to rob the mail this morning and steal his own warrant of arrest."

"Ah, so that's what it was."

"I notified Chief Inspector Shapples yesterday that I had my man under observation, but when I left the Yard the warrant was not complete. The whole thing seemed so simple that he said he'd post it to me, which is quite an irregular proceeding, but one we occasionally indulge in. When it did not come this morning I judged that you had stolen it, and so I obtained a new one to-day. I must say, in fairness to our service, that you have been watched and followed all day and that you would have found it somewhat difficult to make an escape. I did not arrest you before because I did not wish to miss our little dinner this evening, and I also wanted to glean some information about other parties who are still at large. I thought you were fencing very skilfully, and, if you will allow me to say so, I am glad now that I was quite on the wrong tack."

"Inspector," replied the American, "I have not enjoyed such a dinner for a very, very long time, and I'm real glad to have made your acquaintance."

"After this success I hope the authorities will permit you to assist me in unraveling other little troubles in connection with the case before you return to New York. Here's to your good health and prosperity!"

"And yours. Inspector, to say nothing of Mrs. Huggins! My, is n't she a peach!"

"You know, dearie," said Mrs. Huggins, three weeks later, in the private bar of the Staff of Life, to her friend Mrs. O'Neil, "it's a very rum thing about gals. There's my Mag, now. Lord! how she took on when this 'ere case came up. She was going to do this, that, and the other; but when they reely took 'im away, she calmed down like the lamb she is. And now she's already walking out with Sandy Waters, as nice a young feller as you could wish to meet. He's a soldier, you know, an officer; 'e's got all these 'ere stripes on 'is arm. A quartermaster, that's what 'e is; gets 'is perks all over the place. Gets quite a good livin', and when 'e goes, she gets 'er maintenance and a bob a day what 'e allots 'er like, to say nothin' of seven and six for the first child, six shillings for the second, three and six for the third, and three bob apiece for the rest; that is, if the war lasts long enough. They 're as sweet on each other as a couple of gumdrops in a glass bottle."

Mrs. O'Neil blew the froth off the stout.

"It's a wonderful' interestin' case," she said, "what wif all this spyin' and cheatin' and stealin'. Lord! what a narrer escape you 'ad, Mrs. 'Uggins! 'Im comin', too, and stealin' the postman's letters in the mornin'. What a villain!"

Mrs. Huggins coughed, and cleared her throat. Then she looked thoughtfully across her glass and said:

"Well, you know, dearie, it's rather funny about that part. Of course, you know, it's nothing departmental to the case, as they say, or I might 'ave spoken out in court about it; but as a matter of fact, 'e never pinched that letter at all."

Mrs. O'Neil looked aghast, and Mrs. Huggins winked mysteriously.

"No. You see," she whispered, "it was like this 'ere. I was very rushed that mornin', what with the to-do of Mr. Smith's dinner, and that, and I could n't get the b'iler to go. I never take no noospapers now. There 's nothin' in 'em except about this bloomin' war. I takes my 'Reynold's' on Sunday, but as fire-paper that don't last long. Lately I 've taken to usin' these 'ere circulars what come from the sales, you know—spring goods, white sales, and so on. I never looks at 'em. I simply rips 'em open and shoves 'em into the b'iler fire. On that mornin', being 'ard-pressed as it were, I runs up into the 'all, and seein' circulars there, I cops 'old of 'em and runs down to the scullery. I rips 'em open and shoves 'em in. It was not till I got the b'iler goin' that I realized that one of the circulars 'ad a great red sealin'-wax blob on the envelop, and it was all official-like. It was too late then, but I thinks to myself: 'I burnt somethin' I did n't ought to then. That was a summons or somethin'.' Soon after that I 'eard the rumpus up-stairs."

"Lord!" exclaimed Mrs. O'Neil. "You run a risk there, Annie."

"As I say," repeated Mrs. Huggins, "it was n't departmental to the case. There was enough proved against 'im to 'ang 'im in this country and quarter 'im in America without draggin' in a silly old envelop like that."

"Well, I 'ope your Mag 'll be 'appy," said Mrs. O'Neil, wiping her mouth.

"My Mag 'll be all right. Don't you worry," replied Mrs. Huggins.

Solemn-Looking Blokes

At midday on August 15th I stood on the pavement in Cockspur Street and watched the first contingent of American troops pass through London.

I had been attracted thither by the lure of a public "show," by the blare of a band, and by a subconscious desire to pay tribute in my small way to a great people. It was a good day for London, intermittently bright, with great scurrying masses of cumuli overhead, and a characteristic threat of rain, which fortunately held off. Cockspur Street, as you know, is a turning off Trafalgar Square, and I chose it because the crowd was less dense there than in the square itself. By getting behind a group of shortish people and by standing on tiptoe I caught a fleeting view of the faces of nearly every one of the passing soldiers.

London is schooled to shows of this kind. The people gather and wait patiently on the line of route. And then some genial policemen appear and mother the people back into some sort of line, an action performed with little fuss or trouble. Then mounted police appear, headed by some fat official in a cockade hat and with many ribbons on his chest. And some one in the crowd calls out:

"Hullo, Percy! Mind you don't fall off yer 'orse!"

Then the hearers laugh and begin to be on good terms with themselves, for they know that the "show" is coming. Then follows the inevitable band, and we begin to cheer.

It is very easy and natural for a London crowd to cheer. I have heard Kaiser William II cheered in the streets of London! We always cheer our guests, and we love a band and a "show" almost as much as our republican friends across the channel. I have seen royal funerals and weddings, processions in honor of visiting presidents and kings, the return of victorious generals, processions of Canadian, Australian, Indian, French, and Italian troops and bands. I would n't miss these things for worlds. They give color to our social life and accent to our every-day emotions. It is, moreover, peculiarly interesting to observe national traits on a march: the French, with their exuberant élan, throwing kisses to the women as they pass; our own Tommies, who have surprised the world with their gaiety, and keep up a constant ragging intercourse with the crowd and cannot cease from singing; the Indians, who pass like a splendidly carved frieze; the Canadians, who move with a free and independent swing and grin in a friendly way; the Scotch, who carry it off better than any one. But I had never seen American troops, and I was anxious to see how they behaved. I said to myself, "The American is volatile and impressionable, like a child." I had met Americans who within an hour's acquaintance had told me their life-story, given me their views on religion, politics, and art, and invited me to go out to Iowa or Wisconsin or California and spend the summer with them. Moreover, the American above all things is emotional and—may I say it?— sentimental. It would therefore be extremely interesting to see how he came through this ordeal.

The first band passed, and the people were waving flags and handkerchiefs from the windows. We could hear the cheers go up from the great throng in the square. And there at last, sure enough, was Old Glory, with its silken tassels floating in the London breeze, carried by a solemn giant, with another on each side. And then they came, marching in fours, with their rifles at the slope, the vanguard of Uncle Sam's army. And we in Cockspur Street raised a mighty cheer. They were solemn, bronzed men, loose of limb, hard, and strong, with a curious set expression of purpose about them.

Tramp, tramp, tramp, tramp.

And they looked neither to the right nor the left; nor did they look up or smile or apparently take any notice of the cheers we raised. We strained forward to see their faces, and we cried out to them our welcome. Tramp, tramp, tramp, tramp.

They were not all tall; some were short and wiry. Some of the officers were rather elderly and wore horn spectacles. But they did not look at us or raise a smile of response. They held themselves very erect, but their eyes were cast down or fixed upon the back of the man in front of them. There came an interval, and another band, and then Old Glory once more, and we cheered the flag even more than the men. Fully a thousand men passed in this solemn procession, not one of them smiling or looking up. It became almost disconcerting. It was a thing we were not used to. A fellow-cockney near me murmured:

"They 're solemn-looking blokes, ain't they?"

Tramp, tramp, tramp, tramp.

The band blared forth once more, a drum-and-fife corps with a vibrant thrill behind it. We strained forward more eagerly to see the faces of our friends from the New World. We loved it best when the sound of the band had died away and the only music was the steady throb of those friendly boots upon our London streets. And still they did not smile. I had a brief moment of some vague apprehension, as though something could not be quite right. Some such wave, I think, was passing through the crowd. What did it mean?

Tramp, tramp, tramp, tramp.

The cheers died away for a few moments in an exhausted diminuendo. Among those people, racked by three years of strain and suffering, there probably was not one who had not lost some one dear to them. Even the best nerves have their limitation of endurance. Suddenly the ready voice of a woman from the pavement called out:

"God bless you, Sammy!"

And then we cheered again in a different key, and I noticed a boy in the ranks throw back his head and look up. On his face was that expression we see only on the faces of those who know the finer sensibilities—a fierce, exultant joy that is very near akin to tears. And gradually I became aware that on the faces of these grim men was written an emotion almost too deep for expression.

As they passed it was easy to detect their ethnological heritage. There was the Anglo-Saxon type, perhaps predominant; the Celt; the Slav; the Latin; and in many cases definitely the Teuton: and yet there was not one of them that had not something else, who was not pre-eminently a good "United States-man." It was as though upon the anvil of the New World all the troubles of the Old, after being passed through a white-hot furnace, had been forged into something clear and splendid. And they were hurrying on to get this accomplished. For once and all the matter must be settled.

Tramp, tramp, tramp, tramp.

There was a slight congestion, and the body of men near me halted and marked time. A diminutive officer with a pointed beard was walking alone. A woman in the crowd leaned forward and waved an American flag in his face. He saluted, made some kindly remark, and then passed on.

Tramp, tramp, tramp, tramp.

The world must be made safe for democracy.

And I thought inevitably of the story of the Titan myth, of Prometheus, the first real democrat, who held out against the gods because they despised humanity. And they nailed him to a rock, and cut off his eyelids, and a vulture fed upon his entrails.

But Prometheus held on, his line of reasoning being:

"After Uranus came Cronus. After Cronus came Zeus. After Zeus will come other gods."

It is the finest epic in human life, and all the great teachers and reformers who came after told the same story—Christ, Vishnu, Confucius, Mohammed, Luther, Shakspere. The fundamental basis of their teaching was love and faith in humanity. And whenever humanity is threatened, the fires which Prometheus stole from the gods will burn more brightly in the heart of man, and they will come from all quarters of the world.

He is trampling out the vintage where the grapes of wrath are stored;
He hath loosed the fateful lightning of his terrible, swift sword.

There is no quarter, no mercy, to the enemies of humanity. This is no longer a war; it is a crusade. And as I stood on the flags of Cockspur Street I think I understood the silence of those grim men. They seemed to epitomize not merely a nation, not merely a flag, but the unbreakable sanctity of human rights and human life. And I knew that whatever might happen, whatever the powers of darkness might devise, whatever cunning schemes or diabolical plans, or whatever temporary successes they might attain, they would ultimately go down into the dust before "the fateful lightning." "After Zeus will come other gods."

Tramp, tramp, tramp, tramp.

Nothing could live and endure against that steady and irresistible progression. And we know how you can do things, America. We have seen your workshops, your factories, and your engines of peace. And we have seen those young men of yours at the Olympic Games, with their loose, supple limbs, their square, strong faces. When the Spartans, lightly clad, but girt for war, ran across the hills to Athens and, finding the Persian hosts defeated, laughed, congratulated the Athenians, and ran back again—since those days there never were such runners, such athletes, as these boys of yours from Yale and Harvard, Princeton and Cornell.

And so on that day, if we cheered the flag more than we cheered the men, it was because the flag was the symbol of the men's hearts, which were too charged with the fires of Prometheus to trust themselves expression.

At least that is how it appeared to me on that forenoon in Cockspur Street, and I know that later in the day, when I met a casual friend, and he addressed me with the usual formula of the day:

"Any news?"

I was able to say:

"Yes, the best news in the world."

And when he replied:

"What news?"

I could say with all sincerity:

"I have seen a portent. The world is safe for democracy."

Them Others

It is always disturbing to me when things fall into pattern form, when, in fact, incidents of real life dovetail with each other in such a manner as to suggest the shape of a story. A story is a nice, neat little thing, with what is called a "working-up" and a climax, and life is a clumsy, ungraspable thing, very incomplete in its periods, and with a poor sense of climax. In fact, death, which is a very uncertain quantity, is the only definite note it strikes, and even death has an uncomfortable way of setting other things in motion. If, therefore, in telling you about my friend Mrs. Ward, I am driven to the usual shifts of the story-teller, you must believe me that it is because this narrative concerns visions—Mrs. Ward's visions, my visions, and your visions. Consequently I am dependent upon my own poor powers of transcription to mold these visions into shape, and am driven into the position of a story-teller against my will.

The first vision, then, concerns the back view of the Sheldrake Road, which, as you know, butts on to the railway embankment near Dalston Junction station. If you are of an adventurous turn of mind, you will accompany me, and we shall creep up on to the embankment together and look down into these back yards. We shall be liable to a fine of forty shillings, according to a by-law of the railway company, for doing so, but the experience will justify us.

There are twenty-two of these small buff-brick houses huddled together in this road, and there is surely no more certain way of judging not only of the character of the individual inhabitants, but of their mode of life, than by a survey of these somewhat pathetic yards. Is it not, for instance, easy to determine the timid, well-ordered mind of little Miss Porson, the dressmaker at Number 9, by its garden of neat mud paths, with its thin patch of meager grass and the small bed of skimpy geraniums? Cannot one read the tragedy of those dreadful Alleson people at Number 4? The garden is a wilderness of filth and broken bottles, where even the weeds seem chary of establishing themselves. In fact, if we listen carefully, and the trains are not making too much noise, we can hear the shrill crescendo of Mrs. Alleson's voice cursing at her husband in the kitchen, the half-empty gin-bottle between them.

The methodical pushfulness and practicability of young Mr. and Mrs. Andrew MacFarlane is evident at Number 14. They have actually grown a patch of potatoes and some scarlet runners, and there is a chicken-run near the house.

Those irresponsible people, the O'Neals, have grown a bed of hollyhocks, but for the rest the garden is untidy and unkempt. One could almost swear that they were connected in some obscure way with the theatrical profession.

Mrs. Abbot's garden is a sort of playground. It has asphalt paths, always swarming with small and not too clean children, and there are five lines of washing suspended above the mud. Every day seems to be Mrs. Abbot's washing-day. Perhaps she "does" for others. Sam Abbot is certainly a lazy, insolent old rascal, and such always seem destined to be richly fertile. Mrs. Abbot is a pleasant "body," though. The Greens are the swells of the road. George Green is in the grocery line, and both his sons are earning good money, and one daughter has piano lessons. The narrow strip of yard is actually divided into two sections, a flower-garden and a kitchen-garden. They are the only people who have flower-boxes in the front.

Number 8 is a curious place. Old Mr. Bilge lives there. He spends most of his time in the garden, but nothing ever seems to come up. He stands about in his shirt-sleeves, and with a circular paper hat on his head, like a printer. They say he was formerly a corn merchant, but has lost all his money. He keeps the garden very neat and tidy, but nothing seems to grow. He stands there staring at the beds, as though he found their barrenness quite unaccountable.

Number 11 is unoccupied, and Number 12 is Mrs. Ward's.

We now come to an important vision, and I want you to come down with me from the embankment and to view Mrs. Ward's garden from inside, and also Mrs. Ward as I saw her on that evening when I had occasion to pay my first visit.

It had been raining, but the sun had come out. We wandered round the paths together, and I can see her old face now, lined and seamed with years of anxious toil and struggle her long, bony arms, slightly withered, moving restlessly in the direction of snails and slugs.

"Oh dear! oh dear!" she was saying, "what with the dogs and the cats and the snails and the trains, it's wonderful anything comes up at all!"

Mrs. Ward's garden has a character of its own, and I cannot account for it. There is nothing very special growing—a few pansies, a narrow border of London-pride, and several clumps of unrecognizable things that haven't flowered. The grass patch is in only fair order, and at the end of the garden is an unfinished rabbit-hutch. But there is about Mrs. Ward's garden an atmosphere. There is something about it that reflects her placid eye, the calm, somewhat contemplative way she has of looking right through things, as though they didn't concern her too closely; as though, in fact, she were too occupied with her own inner visions.

"No," she said in answer to my query, "we don't mind the trains at all. In fact, me and my Tom we often come out here and sit after supper. And Tom smokes his pipe. We like to hear the trains go by."

She gazed abstractedly at the embankment.

"I like to hear things—going on and that. It's Dalston Junction a little further on. The trains go from there to all parts, right out into the country they do—ever so far. My Ernie went from Dalston."

She added the last in a changed tone of voice. And now perhaps we come to the most important vision of all—Mrs, Ward's vision of "my Ernie."

I ought perhaps to mention that I had never met "my Ernie." I can see him only through Mrs. Ward's eyes. At the time when I met her he had been away at the war for nearly a year. I need hardly say that "my Ernie" was a paragon of sons. He was brilliant, handsome, and incredibly clever. Everything that "my Ernie" said was treasured. Every opinion that he expressed stood. If "my Ernie" liked any one, that person was always a welcome guest. If "my Ernie" disliked any one he was not to be tolerated, however plausible he might appear.

I had seen Ernie's photograph, and I must confess that he appeared a rather weak, extremely ordinary-looking young man; but, then, I would rather trust to Mrs. Ward's visions than to the art of any photographer.

Tom Ward was a mild, ineffectual-looking old man, with something of Mrs. Ward's placidity, but with nothing of her strong individual poise. He had some job in a gas-works. There was also a daughter named Lily, a brilliant person who served in a tea-shop, and sometimes went to theaters with young men. To both husband and daughter Mrs. Ward adopted an affectionate, mothering, almost pitying attitude; but with "my Ernie" it was quite a different thing. I can see her stooping figure and her silver-white hair gleaming in the sun as we came to the unfinished rabbit-hutch, and hear the curious, wistful tones of her voice as she touched it and said:

"When my Ernie comes home—"

The war to her was some unimaginable, but disconcerting, affair centered round Ernie. People seemed to have got into some desperate trouble, and Ernie was the only one capable of getting them out of it. I could not at that time gage how much Mrs. Ward realized the dangers the boy was experiencing. She always spoke with conviction that he would return safely. Nearly every other sentence contained some reference to things that were to happen "when my Ernie comes home." What doubts and fears she had were recognizable only by the subtlest shades in her voice.

When we looked over the wall into the deserted garden next door, she said:

"Oh dear! I'm afraid they 'll never let that place. It's been empty since the Stellings went away. Oh, years ago, before this old war."

It was on the occasion of my second visit that Mrs. Ward told me more about the Stellings. It appeared that they were a German family, of all things! There were a Mr. Stelling, a Mrs. Frow Stelling, and two boys.

Mr. Stelling was a watchmaker, and he came from a place called Bremen. It was a very sad story Mrs. Ward told me. They had been over here only for ten months when Mr. Stelling died, and Mrs. Frow Stelling and the boys went back to Germany.

During the time of the Stellings' sojourn in the Sheldrake Road it appeared that the Wards had seen a good deal of them, and though it would be an exaggeration to say that they ever became great friends, they certainly got through that period without any unpleasantness, and even developed a certain degree of intimacy.

"Allowing for their being foreigners," Mrs. Ward explained, "they were quite pleasant people."

On one or two occasions they invited each other to supper, and I wish my visions were sufficiently clear to envisage those two families indulging this social habit.

According to Mrs. Ward, Mr. Stelling was a kind little man, with a round, fat face. He spoke English fluently, but Mrs. Ward objected to his table manners.

"When my Tom eats," she said, "you don't hear a sound,—I look after that,—but that Mr. Stelling! Oh dear!"

The trouble with Mrs. Stelling was that she could speak only a few words of English, but Mrs. Ward said "she was a pleasant-enough little body," and she established herself quite definitely in Mrs. Ward's affections for the reason that she was so obviously and so passionately devoted to her two sons.

"Oh, my word, though, they do have funny ways, these foreigners!" she continued. "The things they used to eat! Most peculiar! I 've known them eat stewed prunes with hot meat!"

Mrs. Ward repeated, "Stewed prunes with hot meat!" several times, and shook her head, as though this exotic mixture was a thing to be sternly discouraged. But she acknowledged that Mrs. Frow Stelling was in some ways a very good cook; in fact, her cakes were really wonderful, "the sort of thing you can't ever buy in a shop."

About the boys there seemed to be a little divergence of opinion. They were both also fat-faced, and their heads were "almost shaved like convicts'." The elder one wore spectacles and was rather noisy. "My Ernie liked the younger one. Oh, yes, my Ernie said that young Hans was quite a nice boy. It was funny the way they spoke—funny and difficult to understand."

It was very patent that between the elder boy and Ernie, who were of about the same age, there was an element of rivalry which was perhaps more accentuated in the attitude of the mothers than in the boys themselves. Mrs. Ward could find little virtue in this elder boy. Most of her criticism of the family was leveled against him. The rest she found only a little peculiar. She said she had never heard such a funny Christian name as Frow. Florrie she had heard of, and even Flora, but not Froze. I suggested that perhaps Frow might be some sort of title; but she shook her head and said that that was what she was always known as in the Sheldrake Road, "Mrs. Frow Stelling."

Despite Mrs. Ward's lack of opportunity for greater intimacy on account of the language problem, her own fine imaginative qualities helped her a great deal. In one particular she seemed curiously vivid. She gathered an account from one of them—I'm not sure whether it was Mr. Stelling or Mrs. Frow Stelling or one of the boys—of a place they described near their home in Bremen. There was a narrow street of high buildings by a canal, and a little bridge that led over into a gentleman's park. At a point where the canal turned sharply eastward there was a clump of linden-trees where one could go in the summer-time, and under their shade one might sit comfortably and drink light beer and listen to a band that played in the early part of the evening.

Mrs. Ward was curiously clear about that. She said she often thought about Mr. Stelling sitting there after his day's work. It must have been very pleasant tor him, and he seemed to miss this luxury in Dalston more than anything. Once Ernie, in a friendly mood, had taken him into the four-ale bar of The Unicorn, at the corner of the Sheldrake Road, but Mr. Stelling did not seem happy. Ernie acknowledged afterward that it had been an unfortunate evening. The bar had been rather crowded, and there were a man and two women who had all been drinking too much. In any case, Mr. Stelling had been obviously restless there, and he had said afterward:

"It is not that one wishes to drink only—"

And he had shaken his fat little head, and had never been known to visit The Unicorn again.

Mr. Stelling died suddenly of some heart trouble, and Mrs. Ward could not get it out of her head that his last illness was brought about by his disappointment and grief in not being able to go and sit quietly under the linden-trees after his day's work and listen to a band.

"You know, my dear," she said, "when you get accustomed to a thing, it's bad for' you to leave it off."

When poor Mr. Stelling died, Mrs. Frow Stelling was heartbroken, and I have reason to believe that Mrs. Ward went in and wept with her, and in their dumb way they forged the chains of some desperate understanding. When Mrs. Frow Stelling went back to Germany they promised to write to each other. But they never did, and for a very good reason. As Mrs. Ward said, she was "no scholard," and as for Mrs. Frow Stelling, her English was such a doubtful quantity that she probably never got beyond addressing the envelop.

"That was three years ago," said Mrs. Ward. "Them boys must be eighteen and nineteen now."

If I have intruded too greatly into the intimacy of Mrs. Ward's life, one of my excuses must be not that I am "a scholard," but that I am in any case able to read a simple English letter. I was, in fact, on several occasions "requisitioned." When Lily was not at home, some one had to read Ernie's letters out loud. The arrival of Ernie's letters was always an inspiring experience. I might perhaps be in the garden with Mrs. Ward when Tom would come hurrying out to the back and call out:

"Mother! a letter from Ernie!"

And then there would be such excitement and commotion. The first thing was always the hunt for Mrs. Ward's spectacles. They were never where she had put them. Tom would keep on turning the letter over in his hands and examining the postmark, and he would reiterate:

"Well, what did you do with them, Mother?"

At length they would be found in some unlikely place, and she would take the letter tremblingly to the light. I never knew quite how much Mrs. Ward could read. She could certainly read a certain amount. I saw her old eyes sparkling and her tongue moving jerkily between her parted lips, as though she were formulating the words she read, and she would keep on repeating:

"T'ch! T'ch! Oh dear, oh dear, the things he says!"

And Tom, by the door, would say, impatiently:

"Well, what does he say?"

She never attempted to read the letter out loud, but at last she would wipe her spectacles and say:

"Oh, you read it, sir. The things he says!"

They were indeed very good letters of Ernie's, written apparently in the highest spirits. There was never a grumble; not a word. One might gather that he was away with a lot of young bloods on some sporting expedition in which foot-ball, rags, sing-songs, and strange feeds played a conspicuous part. I read a good many of Ernie's letters, and I do not remember that he ever made a single reference to the horrors of war or said anything about his own personal discomforts. The boy must have had something of his mother in him despite the photograph.

And between the kitchen and the yard Mrs. Ward would spend her day placidly content, for Ernie never failed to write. There was sometimes a lapse of a few days, but the letter seldom failed to come every fortnight.

It would be difficult to know what Mrs. Ward's actual conception of the war was. She never read the newspapers, for the reason, as she explained, that "there was nothing in them these days except about this old war." She occasionally dived into Reynolds's newspaper on Sundays to see if there were any interesting law-cases or any news of a romantic character. There was nothing romantic in the war news; it was all preposterous. She did, indeed, read the papers for the first few weeks; but this was for the reason that she had some vague idea that they might contain some account of Ernie's doings. But as they did not, she dismissed them with contempt.

But I found her one night in a peculiarly preoccupied mood. She was out in the garden, and she kept staring abstractedly over the fence into the unoccupied ground next door. It appeared that it had dawned upon her that the war was to do with "these Germans,"—that, in fact, we were fighting the Germans,—and then she thought of the Stellings. Those boys would now be about eighteen and nineteen. They would be fighting, too. They would be fighting against Ernie. This seemed very peculiar.

"Of course," she said, "I never took to that elder boy; a greedy, rough sort of boy he was. But I'm sure my Ernie wouldn't hurt young Hans."

She meditated for a moment as though she were contemplating what particular action Ernie would take in the matter. She knew he didn't like the elder boy, but she doubted whether he would want to do anything very violent to him.

"They went out to a music-hall one night together," she explained, as though a friendship cemented in this luxurious fashion could hardly be broken by an unreasonable display of passion.

It was a few weeks later that the terror suddenly crept into Mrs. Ward's life. Ernie's letters ceased abruptly. The fortnight passed, then three weeks, four weeks, five weeks, and not a word. I do not think that Mrs. Ward's character at any time stood out so vividly as during those weeks of stress. It is true she appeared a little feebler, and she trembled in her movements, while her eyes seemed abstracted, as though all the power in them were concentrated in her ears, alert for the bell or the knock. She started visibly at odd moments, and her imagination was always carrying her tempestuously to the front door, only to answer a milkman or a casual hawker. But she never expressed her fear in words. When Tom came home,—he seemed to have aged rapidly,—he would come bustling out into the garden and cry out tremblingly:

"There ain't been no letter to-day, Mother?"

And she would say quite placidly: "No, not to-day, Tom. It 'll come to-morrow, I expect."

And she would rally him and talk of little things and get busy with his supper. And in the garden I would try to talk to her about her clump of pansies and the latest yarn about the neighbors, and I tried to get between her and the rabbit-hutch, with its dumb appeal of incompletion. And I would notice her staring curiously over into the empty garden next door, as though she were being assailed by some disturbing apprehensions. Ernie would not hurt that eldest boy; but suppose, if things were reversed—There was something inexplicable and terrible lurking in this passive silence.

During this period the old man was suddenly taken very ill. He came home one night with a high temperature, and developed pneumonia. He was laid up for many weeks, and she kept back the telegram that came while he was almost unconscious, and she tended him night and day, nursing her own anguish with a calm face; for the telegram told her that her Ernie was "missing and believed wounded."

I do not know at what period she told the father this news, but it was certainly not till he was convalescent. The old man seemed to sink into a kind of apathy. He sat feebly in front of the kitchen fire, coughing, and making no effort to control his grief. Outside the great trains went rushing by night and day. Things were "going on," but they were all meaningless, cruel.

We made inquiries at the War Office, but they could not amplify the laconic telegram.

Then the winter came on, and the gardens were bleak in the Sheldrake Road. And Lily ran away and married a young tobacconist who was earning twenty-five shillings a week. Old Tom was dismissed from the gas-works. His work was not proving satisfactory. He sat about at home and moped. In the meantime the price of food-stuffs was going up, and coals were a luxury. So in the early morning Mrs. Ward would go off and work for Mrs. Abbot at the wash-tub, and she would earn eight or twelve shillings a week.

It is difficult to know how they managed during those days, but one could see that Mrs. Ward was buoyed up by some poignant hope. She would not give way. Eventually old Tom did get some work to do at a stationer's. The work was comparatively light, and the pay equally so; so Mrs. Ward still continued to work for Mrs. Abbot.

My next vision of Mrs, Ward concerns a certain winter evening. I could not see inside the kitchen, but the old man could be heard complaining. His querulous voice was rambling on, and Mrs. Ward was standing by the door leading into the garden. She had returned from her day's work, and was scraping a pan out into a bin near the door. A train shrieked by, and the wind was blowing a fine rain against the house. Suddenly she stood up and looked up at the sky; then she pushed back her hair from her brow, and frowned at the dark house next door; then she turned and said:

"Oh, I don't know, Tom; if we 've got to do it, we must do it. If them others can stand it, we can stand it. Whatever them others can do, we can do."

And then my visions jump rather wildly, and the war becomes to me epitomized in two women: one in this dim doorway, in our obscure suburb of Dalston, scraping out a pan; and the other, perhaps in some dark, high house near a canal on the outskirts of Bremen. Them others! These two women silently enduring, and the trains rushing by, and all the dark, mysterious forces of the night operating on them equivocally.

Poor Mrs. Frow Stelling! Perhaps those boys of hers are "missing, believed killed." Perhaps they are killed for certain. She is as much outside "the things going on" as Mrs. Ward. Perhaps she is equally as patient, as brave.

Mrs. Ward entered the kitchen, and her eyes were blazing with a strange light as she said:

"We 'll hear to-morrow, Tom. And if we don't hear to-morrow, we 'll hear the next day. And if we don't hear the next day, we 'll hear the day after. And if we don't—if we don't never hear—again—if them others can stand it, we can stand it, I say."

And then her voice broke, and she cried a little; for endurance has its limitations, and the work was hard at Mrs. Abbot's.

And the months went by, and she stooped a little more as she walked, and some one had thrown a cloth over the rabbit-hutch, with its unfinished roof. Mrs. Ward was curiously retrospective. It was useless to tell her of the things of the active world. She listened politely, but she did not hear. She was full of reminiscences of Ernie's and Lily's childhood. She recounted again and again the story of how Ernie, when he was a little boy, ordered five tons of coal from a coal merchant to be sent to a girls' school in Dalston highroad. She described the coal-carts arriving in the morning, and the consternation of the head-mistress.

"Oh dear! oh dear!" she said, "the things he did!"

She did not talk much of the Stellings, but one day she said meditatively:

"Mrs. Frow Stelling thought a lot of that boy Hans. So she did of the other, as far as that goes. It's only natural-like, I suppose."

As time went on, Tom Ward lost all hope. He said he was convinced that the boy was killed. Having arrived at this conclusion, he seemed to become more composed. He gradually began to accustom himself to the new point of view. But with Mrs. Ward the exact opposite was the case. She was convinced that the boy was alive, but she suffered terribly.

There came a time—it was in early April—when one felt that the strain could not last. She seemed to lose all interest in the passing world, and lived entirely within herself. Even the arrival of Lily's baby did not rouse her. She looked at the child queerly, as though she doubted whether any useful or happy purpose was served by its appearance. It was a boy.

Despite her averred optimism, she lost her tremulous sense of apprehension when the bell rang or the front door was tapped. She let the milkman and even the postman wait.

When she spoke, it was invariably of things that happened years ago. Sometimes she talked about the Stellings, and on one Sunday she made a strange pilgrimage out to Finchley, and visited Mr. Stelling's grave. I don't know what she did there, but she returned looking very exhausted and unwell. As a matter of fact, she was unwell for days after this visit, and she suffered violent twinges of rheumatism in her legs.

I now come to my most unforgettable vision of Mrs. Ward. It was a day at the end of April, and warm for the time of year. I was standing in the garden with her, and it was nearly dark. A goods-train had been shunting, and making a great deal of noise in front of the house, and at last had disappeared. I had not been able to help noticing that Mrs. Ward's garden was curiously neglected for the time of year. The grass was growing on the paths, and the snails had left their silver trail over all the fences.

I was telling her a rumor I had heard about the railway porter and his wife at Number 23, and she seemed fairly interested; for she had known John Hemsley, the porter, fifteen years ago, when Ernie was a baby. There were two old, broken Windsor chairs out in the garden, and on one was a zinc basin in which were some potatoes. She was peeling them, as Lily and her husband were coming to supper. By the kitchen door was a small sink. When she had finished the potatoes, she stood up and began to pour the water down the sink, taking care not to let the skins go, too. I was noticing her old, bent back, and her long, bony hands gripping the sides of the basin, when suddenly a figure came limping round the bend of the house from the side passage, and two arms were thrown round her waist, and a voice said:

"Mind them skins don't go down the sink. Mother. They 'll stop it up."

As I explained to Ernie afterward, it was an extremely foolish thing to do. If his mother had had anything wrong with her heart, it might have been very serious. There have been many cases of people dying from the shock of such an experience.

As it was, she merely dropped the basin and stood there trembling like a leaf, and Ernie laughed loud and uproariously. It must have been three or four minutes before she could regain her speech, and then all she could manage to say was:

"Ernie! My Ernie!"

And the boy laughed, and ragged his mother, and pulled her into the house, and Tom appeared, and stared at his son, and said feebly:

"Well, I never!"

I don't know how it was that I found myself intruding upon the sanctity of the inner life of the Ward family that evening. I had never had a meal there before, but I felt that I was holding a sort of watching brief over the soul and body of Mrs. Ward. I had had a little medical training in my early youth, and this may have been one of the reasons that prompted me to stay.

When Lily and her husband appeared, we sat down to a meal of mashed potatoes and onions stewed in milk, With bread and cheese; and very excellent it was. Lily and her husband took the whole thing in a boisterous, high-comedy manner that fitted in with the mood of Ernie. Old Tom sat there staring at his son, and repeating at intervals:

"Well, I never!"

Mrs. Ward hovered round the boy's plate. Her eyes divided their time between his plate and his face, and she hardly spoke all the evening.

Ernie's story was remarkable enough. He told it disconnectedly and rather incoherently. There were moments when he rambled in a rather peculiar way, and sometimes he stammered, and seemed unable to frame a sentence. Lily's husband went out to fetch some beer to celebrate the joyful occasion, and Ernie drank his in little sips and spluttered. The boy must have suffered considerably. He had a wound in the abdomen, and another in the right forearm that for a time had paralyzed him.

As far as I could gather, his story was this:

He and a platoon of men had been ambushed and had had to surrender. When being sent back to a base, three of them tried to escape from the train, which had been held up at night. He did not know what had happened to the other two men, but it was on this occasion that he received his abdominal wound at the hands of a guard.

He had then been sent to some infirmary, where he was fairly well treated; but as soon as his wound had healed a little, he had been suddenly sent to some fortress prison, presumably as a punishment. He had n't the faintest idea how long he had been confined there. He said it seemed like fifteen years. It was probably nine months. He had solitary confinement in a cell, which was like a small lavatory. He had fifteen minutes' exercise every day in a yard with some other prisoners, who were Russians, he thought. He spoke to no one. He used to sing and recite in his cell, and there were times when he was quite convinced that he was "off his chump." He said he had lost "all sense of everything" when he was suddenly transferred to another prison. Here the conditions were somewhat better, and he was made to work. He said he wrote six or seven letters home from there, but received no reply. The letters certainly never reached Dalston. The food was execrable, but a big improvement on the dungeon. He was there only a few weeks when he and some thirty other prisoners were suddenly sent to work on the land at a kind of settlement. He said that the life there would have been tolerable if it had n't been for the fact that the commandant was an absolute brute. The food was worse than in the prison, and they were punished severely for the most trivial offenses.

It was here, however, that he met a sailor named Martin, a royal naval reservist, an elderly, thick-set man with a black beard and only one eye. Ernie said that this Martin "was an artist. He wangled everything. He had a genius for getting what he wanted. He would get a beefsteak out of a stone." In fact, it was obvious that the whole of Ernie's narrative was colored by his vision of Martin. He said he 'd never met such a chap in his life. He admired him enormously, and he was also a little afraid of him.

By some miraculous means peculiar to sailors, Martin acquired a compass. Ernie hardly knew what a compass was, but the sailor explained to him that it was all that was necessary to take you straight to England. Ernie said he "had had enough escaping. It didn't agree with his health"; but so strong was his faith and belief in Martin that he ultimately agreed to try with him.

He said Martin's method of escape was the coolest thing he 'd ever seen. He planned it all beforehand. It was the fag-end of the day, and the whistle had blown, and the prisoners were trooping back across a potato-field. Martin and Ernie were very slow. They lingered apparently to discuss some matter connected with the soil. There were two sentries in sight, one near them, and the other perhaps a hundred yards away. The potato-field was on a slope, and at the bottom of the field were two lines of barbed-wire entanglements. The other prisoners passed out of sight, and the sentry near them called out something, probably telling them to hurry up. They started to go up the field when suddenly Martin staggered and clutched his throat. Then he fell over backward and began to have an epileptic fit. Ernie said it was the realest thing he'd ever seen. One sentry ran up, at the same time whistling to his comrade. Ernie released Martin's collar-band and tried to help him. Both the sentries approached, and Ernie stood back. He saw them bending over the prostrate man when suddenly a most extraordinary thing happened. Both their heads were brought together with fearful violence. One fell completely senseless, but the other staggered forward and blindly groped for his rifle.

When Ernie told this part of the story he kept dabbing his forehead with his handkerchief.

"I never seen such a man as Martin, I don't think," he said. "Lord! he had a fist like a leg of mutton. He laid 'em out neatly on the grass, took off their coats and most of their other clothes, and flung 'em over the barbed-wire, and then swarmed over like a cat. I had more difficulty, but he got me across, too, somehow. Then we carted the clothes away to the next line.

"We got up into a wood that night, and Martin draws out his compass, and he says: 'We 've got a hundred and seven miles to do in night-shifts, cully. And if we make a slip, we 're shot as safe as knife.' It sounded the maddest scheme in the world, but I somehow felt that Martin would get through it. The only thing that saved me was that—that I didn't have to think. I simply left everything to him. If I'd started thinking, I should have gone mad. I had it fixed in my mind: 'Either he does it or he doesn't do it. I can't help it.' I reely don't remember much about that journey. It was all a dream, like. We did all our travelin' at night by compass, and hid by day. Neither of us had a word of German. But, Gawd's truth! that man Martin was a marvel! He turned our trousers inside out, and made 'em look like ordinary laborers' trousers. He disappeared the first night, and came back with some other old clothes. We lived mostly on raw potatoes we dug out of the ground with our hands, but not always. One night he came back with a fowl, which he cooked in a hole in the earth, making a fire with a flint and some dry stuff he pinched from a farm. I believe Martin could have stole an egg from under a hen without her noticing it. He was the coolest card there ever was. Of course there was a lot of trouble one way and another. It wasn't always easy to find wooded country or protection of any sort. We often ran into people, and they stared at us, and we shifted our course. But I think we were only addressed three or four times by men, and then Martin's methods were the simplest in the world. He just looked sort of blank for a moment, then knocked them clean out, and bolted. Of course they were after us all the time, and it was this constant tacking and shifting ground that took so long. Fancy! he never had a map, you know; nothing but the compass. We didn't know what sort of country we were coming to—nothing. We just crept through the night like cats. I believe Martin could see in the dark. He killed a dog one night with his hands; it was necessary."

It was impossible to discover from Ernie how long this amazing journey lasted; the best part of two months, I believe. He was himself a little uncertain with regard to many incidents whether they were true or whether they were hallucinations. He suffered greatly from his wound and had periods of feverishness. But one morning he said Martin began "prancing." He seemed to develop some curious sense that they were near the Dutch frontier. And then, according to Ernie, "a cat wasn't in it with Martin."

He was very mysterious about the actual crossing. I gathered that there had been some "clumsy" work with sentries. It was at that time that Ernie got a bullet through his arm. When he got to Holland he was very ill. It was not that the wound was a very serious one, but, as he explained:

"Me blood was in a bad state. I was nearly down and out."

He was very kindly treated by some Dutch sisters in a convent hospital. He was delirious for a long time, and when he became more normal, they wanted to communicate with his people in England; but this did n't appeal to the dramatic sense of Ernie.

"I thought I'd spring a surprise-packet on you," he said, grinning.

We asked about Martin, but Ernie said he never saw him again. He went away while Ernie was delirious, and they said he had gone to Rotterdam to take ship somewhere. He thought Holland was a dull place.

During the relation of this narrative my attention was divided between watching the face of Ernie and the face of Ernie's mother. I am quite convinced that she did not listen to the story at all. She never took her eyes from his face, and although her tongue was following the flow of his remarks, her mind was occupied with the vision of Ernie when he was a little boy and when he ordered five tons of coal to be sent to the girls' school.

When he had finished she said:

"Did you meet either of them young Stellings?"

Ernie laughed rather uproariously, and said "No," he didn't have the pleasure of renewing their acquaintance.

On his way home, it appeared, he had presented himself at headquarters, and after a medical examination had received his notice of discharge.

"So now you 'll be able to finish the rabbit-hutch," said Lily's husband, and we all laughed again, with the exception of Mrs. Ward.

I found her later standing alone in the garden. It was a warm spring night. There was no moon, but the sky appeared restless with its burden of trembling stars. She had an old shawl drawn round her shoulders, and she stood there very silent, with her arms crossed.

"Well, this is splendid news, Mrs. Ward," I said.

She started a little and coughed and pulled the shawl closer round her. She said very faintly:

"Yes, sir."

I don't think she was really aware of me. She still appeared immersed in the contemplation of her inner visions. Her eyes settled upon the empty house next door, and I thought I detected the trail of a tear glistening on her cheeks. I lighted my pipe. We could hear Ernie and Lily and Lily's husband still laughing and talking inside.

"She used to make a very good puddin'," Mrs. Ward said suddenly, at random. "Dried fruit inside, and that. My Ernie liked it very much."

Somewhere away in the distance, probably outside The Unicorn, some one was playing a cornet. A train crashed by and disappeared, leaving a trail of foul smoke that obscured the sky. The smoke cleared slowly away. I struck another match to light my pipe.

It was quite true. On each side of her cheek a tear had trickled. She was trembling a little, worn out by the emotions of the evening.

There was a moment of silence unusual for Dalston.

"It's all very—perplexin', and that," she said quietly.

And then I knew for certain that in that great hour of her happiness her mind was assailed by strange and tremulous doubts. She was thinking of "them others" a little wistfully. She was doubting whether one could rejoice, when the thing became clear and actual to one, without sending out one's thoughts into the dark garden to "them others" who were suffering, too. And she had come out into this little, meager yard at Dalston and gazed through the mist and smoke upward to the stars because she wanted peace intensely; and so she sought it within herself, because she knew that real peace is a thing which concerns the heart alone.

So I left her standing there and went my way, for I knew that she was wiser than I.

To-morrow You Will be King

To-morrow you will be king.

This is the best and most highly paid job that I give out. You will have an enormous salary, and you will be able to buy anything you like to eat or drink, but you must wear the clothes that I give you. There will be several hundred suits, and you must wear them on occasions as I dictate. You must always be thinking of ME and my CONSTITUTION (spelled in very large capitals), and you must not have any ideas of your own. You may think, but you must not express your thoughts. You must not have any likes or dislikes, any prejudices, any bias, or any political thought.

"Above all, you must not marry whom you like. I will find you a wife. You see, I was once a slave, as you will be to-morrow, and I like to keep you, although you are expensive to me, because you remind me of that time; or, rather, you bring home to me how I have developed, how I have become free, and I like to feel this power that I, a People (with a very large P), may even keep one slave myself, may even be a tyrant when the mood comes over me. For I rejoice in you, and as you pass me in the street I will take off my hat and bow to you, and when you deign to acknowledge me, I will cheer and cry, 'God save the King!'

"To-morrow and every day after I shall introduce you to hundreds and hundreds of people. You will not find them interesting, in fact you will find them mostly tedious and dull, but you must remember them all—all their names and faces and many facts concerning them, so that in after years, if you meet one of them, you must be ready to say, 'Ah, Mr. Brown, how is your youngest son getting on in Nicaragua?' You must be very careful to remember that it is the youngest son and that it is Nicaragua. If you ask how his eldest son is getting on in Fiji, and his eldest son is dead and had not even been to Fiji, you will estrange

Brown, and I value Brown very highly. He supports the exchequer of one of my greatest parties. I shall expect this of you. It is what I am pleased to call 'tact.' If you meet others, and you look into their eyes, and they seem sympathetic to you, you must not treat them with more cordiality than those to whom you take an aversion.

"You must worship in the church established by my prelates, and considered best for you, and you must be strict in your observances. Every day there will be many papers for you to sign, but fortunately for you, you need not read them, for you must sign them in any case. And when you open my house of government you must read a speech. This speech will be written for you by some one you won't know, and will be printed in bold type, so that it will not be difficult to read.

"This holds good with every public act of yours. I try to make it as easy for you as possible, so that you have no personal worry or responsibility. You must not even refer to yourself as I; you must say 'we.' This does not mean that there is more than one of you, but it gives you emphasis, and lends point to the phrase, 'Le roi est mort. Vive le roi!'

"You may have relaxation,—that is to say, you may have change of scene and to a certain extent change of society,—but you must never deviate by a hair's-breadth from these restrictions that I have laid down. Into my life you will bring color, history, pageantry, and a sense of form. For these things I am prepared to pay you well and to stand by you.

"When your day is finished and you say your prayers and retire to bed, in the silent watches of the night you may have whatever thoughts you like. Of course I should prefer you to think of ME and my CONSTITUTION, but I shall not exact that from you, provided your thoughts do not color your actions of the preceding day. Now go, sire, for to-morrow you will be king."

Tuez! Tuez!

They only who build on Ideas, build for Eternity.—Emerson

It is many years now since I knew you, Anna. We used to meet on certain fine mornings in the gardens of the Tuileries. I don't think we had ever been introduced, but we were great friends. I was quite a man already; nearly sixteen, in fact. I don't know how old you were, Anna, you were always such a baffling mixture of motherliness and sheer infancy. I remember you now in your plaid frock, with your pigtail tied with a large black bow, your chubby face, and your shining eyes. Life was simply a tremendous business to you. You used to arrive encumbered by two brothers, a bull-dog, a nurse with a real baby, a toy pram with two unreal babies, one plain, the other colored, a large kite, some colored picture-books, and occasionally a father. Once in the gardens you would shake off these encumbrances, or, if you did not entirely shake them off, you dominated them. Your vitality was irresistible, your laughter contagious, your immediate power over men and women, and even small boys, a thing not to be denied. And there were so many important things to be done in the gardens, and all to be done quickly, tempestuously, and at the same time. Action, invention, romance tumbled over one another in the terrific fulfilment of those crowded hours.

I was your slave from the first, Anna. You told me frankly all about yourself as we sat upon the grass under the chestnut-trees. You told me all about your brothers and your nurse and your bull-dog and your kite and your father and the two dolls, Iris and Daphne (I am sure you remember Daphne, the colored one), and about your home in Connecticut, embellishing it with vivid stories about a mule and a colored gardener, and Aunt Alice and Uncle Ted and popcorn and a dandy canoe you and your brothers had upon the lake at home, where you played redskins and cow-boys. I was breathless under the spell of these epic adventures. Sometimes I was allowed to release the slack as you ran with the kite. In more favored moments I was allowed to run with the kite myself. So great was your power over me that I even humbled my manly pride by making a patchwork quilt for Daphne, that the colored darling should sleep peacefully in the shade while we sought more stirring adventures in the remote parts of the gardens.

It was in connection with this that the great and tragic episode occurred. I am writing this after all these years in the hope that you may remember it. In one corner of the gardens a group of small and rather dirty boys used to congregate. One of their favorite amusements was to bring an old egg-box stuffed with straw, which served as a cage wherein were kept some half-dozen white mice. The boys would set this on the ground and then release the mice and play with them. They would sometimes let the whole lot go for a considerable distance, and then would follow a round-up. I recollect how intensely interested you were in the white mice, but you always looked upon the "round-up" with some misgiving. The boys would shriek, and chivvy the mice until the wretched things were in a perfect state of panic. One day you felt it incumbent upon you to address them on the subject, and you told them they ought not to do it, and that it was very cruel to frighten dumb creatures. The boys were quite surprised and cowed by your outburst for the moment; but I fear that that devilish streak of cruelty and perversity which lurks in the breast of nearly every small boy was only whipped to a finer point of reaction by your tirade, for on the following day I have the idea that they were lying in wait for us. In any case, when we approached there was such a yelling and shouting and rushing hither and thither that all the Apaches from the Paris prisons might have been let loose. I observed your face light up with a sudden passion, and you rushed forward into the group, calling out:

"Arrêtez!"

You singled out the biggest boy, who was leaping backward and forward over a mouse, and clutched the tail of his coat. And then the tragedy happened. Coming down before he intended to, he brought his heel right down on to the hind quarters of the mouse. It was not a moment for sweet reasonableness. You, with tears of passion in your eyes, screamed:

"You little devil!"

You managed to seize a handful of his face, and push him over backward. And the boy jumped up and kicked your shins. In truly heroic fashion I knocked the boy down again and held him there (I suppose I must remind you that I was much bigger than he was). And then the other boys collected, and the pandemonium became indescribable. One of them pulled your hair, but you soon dealt satisfactorily with him, and they all talked and gesticulated at once. Fortunately, the majority of them were more immediately concerned with rounding up the other mice, which by this time had got a long way off. And your attention was concentrated on the wounded mouse. You looked at it with horror. It was obviously past recall. Both its back legs were broken and its body crushed. It was dying. You wrung your hands.

"Kill it!" you said to me, peremptorily.

And then came to me one of those weak moments which I suppose we are all prone to, and which we ever afterward regret. I blinked at the mouse hopelessly, but I simply could n't bring myself to kill it. You looked at the other boys and stamped your feet.

"Tuez! tuez!" you exclaimed.

But the big boy, whom by this time I had let go, merely broke out into a torrent of incomprehensible argot, and the others were still busy catching the other mice. I observed you glance desperately around. Suddenly you picked up a piece of board that had come off the egg-box. Your face was white and set. Your movements were deliberate and tense. You knelt on the grass above the mouse, and the idea occurred to me, ridiculously perhaps, that at that moment you looked like Joan of Arc kneeling at prayer, her head bent over her sword. And then you killed the mouse. You killed it thoroughly.

You arose without a word, and your face was still pale and set, and you strode away across the grass. I followed you, and the boys followed me, talking volubly. At length, I remember, I gave them a franc. I salved my conscience with the reflection that a white mouse must have a monetary value, and that we might have been indirectly responsible for its loss. If we had not interfered it would probably have had a longer and more harassed existence. In any case, the boys left us apparently satisfied.

When we were out of sight of them, you suddenly sat down on the grass and cried. And you cried and cried and cried. And, like the booby I was, all I could say was:

"Anna, don't cry! Anna! Anna!"

After a time you sat up and wiped your eyes.

"It 's all right," you said. Then you got up, and we walked on. I felt curiously self-conscious and ashamed. I was aware of not having played so glorious a part in the morning's proceedings as I should have liked; moreover, I felt that you had gone beyond me. You had proved yourself a more competent, a more advanced being. I had disappointed you, and you might never again give me your complete confidence.

However, at the exit to the gardens, where we met nurse, you were quite yourself again. Do you remember all this, Anna? You told nurse that you had had "a dandy time." And when we parted you gave me the old smile, and with a malicious twinkle you added, "Mornin', Mr. Hayseed!"

I know all about that, Anna. I am slow-going and old-fashioned. When I find the world tumbling to pieces I am paralyzed by it, and I yearn for you with your impulse and your genius of youth. The years have come and gone since I saw you. I even doubt whether you would remember me, but I am sure you would remember the incident of the white mice. In these days the gardens of the Tuileries themselves seem shut to me forever, and the world is peopled with querulous old men. Old dynasties tremble and crumble up. Political intrigues reap the fruit of their own sowing. Everything becomes more involved and more difficult. Secret treaties are forged by the few, and quite reasonably repudiated by the many. The old make the laws, and the young pay the price. And how splendidly, how loyally, they do it! And it is always that—the old in their secret chambers, scheming, controlling, and shaking their heads, and the young dying unquestioningly out in the open field, believing. For the young always believe, and the old always doubt.

And if in these days, Anna, I am driven to think of you, it is for a very definite reason. It concerns you and it concerns your country. The Old World is rocking in a death-grip. Everything is thrown into the crucible of hate. The horror of these days is borne only because there lurks in the heart of man a subconscious belief that the horror is to prove a solution; that all the troubles of old days, that all differences and antagonisms, are to vanish. The sword of Damocles will be indeed a myth. If I think of you so intently it is because I am perplexed and worried, and I long for the sound of a young voice again. Let me tell you, for I know that you will understand. I have listened to them all these sages of the Eastern World. And they are very wise and knowing, very cunning and very circumspect; but when it comes to the great thing, the thing which touches all our hearts, they shake their heads.

"No," they say lugubriously. "There always have been wars and there always will be wars."

And when I argue with them, they are so recondite, so full of worldly wisdom. And they quote this act and that act and multiply historical precedents. They speak ponderously of "our national responsibilities," "our ancient rights and privileges"; they crush me with their weight of logic. From across the water I hear the thunder of the guns and the reiteration of the ominous phrases, "The German god," "The German sword." "The German peace." And nearer at home I am further depressed by the arguments of our sages.

"What?" they say, "a league of the nations! An idle term! How could such a thing be worked? Should every nation elect an equal number of delegates? Is the British Empire and all that it entails, embodying a population of four hundred million souls, to be on a par with, let us say, the sovereign state of Bogota, which has a million souls and mostly poets!"

And the politicians' contempt for poets is driven home by that contemptuous shrug.

"There would be no way," they say, "of regulating or controlling such a league. Why, some quite backward states might outvote the British, the French, and the United States! There always have been wars and there always will be wars." I remember it was in such a state of bewilderment as this, and it was in another garden not very far from where I live, that on an evening just as the sun was going down I thought of you again. I had read for the first time some words by a man who will one day be very dear to all the world. He is the President of your country. I was distressed and troubled. The problems and anxieties of national life seemed more and more involved and insoluble, the men in power more rigid and inflexible; and suddenly, as I read the words of President Wilson, I realized that here at last was a man who stood apart from his fellows. Amidst the bitter recrimination of national antagonisms, clear-cut through the chopped logic of the politician, he at least seemed to see things clearly with the eyes of a child. While the others were shouting of "The German god" or of "their national aspirations," he suddenly appeared in the due order of things and spoke quite simply of men and ideas. If he spoke of his country at all, it was only as a medium for the advancement of men, for the freedom of their ideas, for the liberty of their thought. One felt at once that one was in the presence of something big and fundamental, without malice, without ulterior motive, without political intrigue or imperial ambition. And when I read his words, I thought of you, and I thought of America as I shall always think of her, as of a child with shining eyes, disturbed in the pursuit of splendid dreams, quick to grasp realities, quick to act, and quick to forgive. And when the terrible business of killing the mouse has got to be done, it will be done quickly, relentlessly, thoroughly, and though one may weep for the sheer horror of it, the day will come when the tears will be wiped away, and one may smile again in the recognition of the fact that there was no alternative.

And the Old World is waiting for you, for it will not believe, and it knows that you will believe, for you alone have the masterful genius of youth, unaware of perils and difficulties, but with eyes set upon the clear horizon you have set out to reach. And in these days, amidst the maelstrom of conflicting opinion of these wise men of the Eastern World, all who love humanity, all who believe in its ultimate destiny toward a better order of society, are driven to turn their eyes more and more to the west. For the turn of the Western World has come, a world where everything is more fluid and free, where everything is possible and hopeful; in short, the world of youth. It was a Western philosopher, Ralph Waldo Emerson, who said:

Society is an illusion to the young citizen. It lies before him in rigid repose, with certain names, men, and institutions rooted like oak-trees in the centre, round which all arrange themselves the best they can. But the old statesman knows that Society is fluid; there are no such roots and centres; but any particle may suddenly become the centre of the movement, and compel the system to gyrate round it.

Emerson may say "the old statesman," but he is essentially the old statesman of the Western World; that is to say, he speaks with the authority of youth. And in these days how terribly we want to believe this, that "some particle may become the center of the movement," that some new hope, some free and novel expression of human ideas, may compel "the whole system to gyrate round it." And that is why we turn with breathless expectancy to the Western World, for it is from there that this new star should rise, guiding the stumbling feet of men to the manger where a new birth will prove to them the salvation of their wavering beliefs. Some little thing may fire this sudden spark; the words of a President, the mood of a congress, an article in a newspaper, some grim material necessity producing a climax of horror, the rise of a world-preacher, the tears of a woman. Whatever it is, it will come, this little point round which the ultimate solutions will revolve. And there is no one I would rather have as a leader in these days than this President of yours; for he reminds me of you, Anna, when you ran with flashing eyes among the boys, and when you knelt there looking like Joan of Arc, and calling out:

"Tuez! tuez!"

And forever after one will weep at the terror of that memory; but the heart is uplifted, and the soul of man made stronger and freer.

Many who play an important part in my life come and go, and I see them no more. And you are one of them, Anna. And in these days I like to think of you. I like to think of you married and surrounded by many fine and "real" children. Perhaps you have sons in France and Flanders, and in that case my heart goes out to you. I know what a mother you will be, and I know that, whatever happens, you will be fine and splendid, strong and courageous, "a mother of men," doing your best, believing in the best, the equipoise of your faith untouched by trouble or anxiety. And on the day when the sun once more looks down serenely on those fair fields now stricken with the horrors of war, I can see those eyes of yours shining with a thankfulness and a wistful pity almost too great to bear, and I can almost hear that mellow voice as you look up at me maliciously, saying "Mornin', Mr, Hayseed!"

In The Way Of Business

As the large, thick-set man with the red face, the bushy mustache, and the very square chin swung round on his swivel chair, at the great roll-top desk with its elaborate arrangements of telephones, receivers, and electric buttons, he conveyed to the little mild-eyed man waiting on a chair by the door the sense of infinite power.

And surely it must be a position requiring singular gifts and remarkable capacity. For was this not Dollbones, the house famous throughout the civilized world for supplying trimmings, gimp, embroidery, buttons, and other accessories to nearly every retail furnisher in England and the colonies? and was not this Mr. Godfrey Hylam, the London manager? To hold such a position a man must have not only brains, and an infinite capacity for work and driving power, but he must have character, a genius for judging people and making quick decisions.

"Almost like a general," thought the mild-eyed man by the door. He had waited fifty minutes in the outer office for his interview, and on being at length shown in, had been told to "sit down a minute." This minute had been protracted into thirty-five minutes, but it was very interesting to watch the great man grappling with the myriad affairs that came whispering through the wires, and giving sharp instructions to the two flurried clerks who sat in the same office, or dictating to the young lady stenographer who sat furtively on a small chair by his side scribbling into a book with a fountain-pen.

"She looks ill and worried," thought the little man. He was indulging in a dreamy speculation on the girl's home life, when he was suddenly pulled up by the percussion of Mr. Hylam's voice. He realized that the great man was speaking to him. He was saying:

"Let's see, what's your name?"

"Thomas Pinwell, sir," he answered, and stood up. "What name?" repeated the big man.

"Pinwell-Thomas Pinwell," he said in a rather louder voice.

Mr. Hylam looked irritably among some papers and sighed. He then continued dictating a letter to the stenographer. When that was finished he got up, and went out of the room. He was absent about ten minutes, and then came hurrying in with some more papers. He called out as he walked:

"Jackson, have you got that statement from Jorrocks, Musgrove & Bellwither?"
One of the clerks jumped up and said: "I'll find it, sir."

The clerk took some time to do this, and in the meanwhile Mr. Hylam dictated another report to the young lady. Then the clerk brought the statement, and he and Mr. Hylam discussed it at some length. He gave the clerk some further instructions, which were twice interrupted by the telephone bell. When this was finished, Mr. Hylam again caught sight of the little man by the door. He looked at him with surprise, and said:

"Let's see, what's your name?"

"Pinwell-Thomas Pinwell, sir," he answered patiently.

Mr. Hylam again sighed and fingered a lot of papers in pigeon-holes. At that moment there was a knock, and a boy in buttons entered and said:

"There's Mr. Curtis, of Curtis, Tonks & Curtis, called."

"Oh!" exclaimed Mr. Hylam. "Yes. All right. Er-ask him to come in. I want to see him." He turned to the telephone, and asked someone to put him on to someone else, and while waiting with the receiver to his ear, his eye once more caught sight of the little man by the door. He called out to him:

"Oh!-er-just wait outside a minute, Mr.—er—Hullo! is that you, Thomson?"

Finding himself temporarily dismissed, Mr. Pinwell took up his hat and went into the outer office. There was a tall, elderly man with a fur-lined overcoat standing there, and he was immediately shown in. He remained with Mr. Hylam just one hour. At the end of that time, one of the directors called and went out to lunch with Mr. Hylam. A clerk gave Mr. Pinwell the tip that he had better call back about four O'clock. He said he would do so. He had had thirty years' experience in the furnishing trade, and he knew that "business was business" One had to be patient, to conform to its prescripts. A gentleman like Mr. Hylam lived under continual pressure. He was acting according to his conscience in the best interests of the firm. One had to take one's chance with him. After all, it would be very nice to get the job. He had been out so long, and he was not so young as he used to be. He thought of his placid wife and the two children. They were indeed getting into a very penurious state. He understood that the salary would be thirty shillings per week and a small royalty on the sales. Not a princely emolument but it would make all the difference. Besides, what might not the royalties amount to? If he worked hard and energetically he might make between two and three pounds per week who knows? He went into an aerated bread shop and had a cup of tea and a piece of seed cake and read the morning paper. He stayed there as long as he dare, and then went for a stroll round the streets. At four o 'clock precisely he presented himself at the managerial office at Dollbones once more. Mr. Hylam had not returned. They expected him every minute. There were five other people waiting to see him. At half-past four Mr. Hylam came in, smoking a cigar. He was accompanied by another gentleman. They walked right through the waiting crowd and went into the inner office and shut the door. As a matter of fact, Mr, Pinwell did not see the manager at all that day. So great was the congestion of business in the trimming, gimp, embroidery, and button business that afternoon that he was advised by one of the least aggressive clerks, at about a quarter to six, to try his luck in the morning. It was a quarter-past three on the following afternoon that he eventually obtained his interview with Mr. Hylam, and it was from his point of view entirely satisfactory. Mr. Hylam said:

"Let's see. You told me your name?"

"Yes, sir," he answered." Thomas Pinwell."

Mr. Hylam seemed at last to find the papers he desired. He said: "Er-just come here. Show me your references."

Mr. Pinwell approached the great desk deferentially. On it was a chart of London with one section shaded red. Mr. Hylam read the references carefully and then asked one or two searching questions. At last he said:

"Well, now, look here. This is your section. Go to Mr. Green, and he will give you the cards and samples. Then go to Rodney in the Outer London department upstairs, and he will give you a list of several hundred furnishing houses with the names of the buyers and a few particulars. Everything else you must find out. The salary is thirty shillings a week and two per cent, on sales completed. Settlement monthly. Good-day, Mr.—er—"

He turned to the telephone, and Mr. Pin-well's heart beat rapidly. He had really got a job again! As he walked to the door he had a vision of the expression of delight on his wife's face as he told her the news. He visualized a certain day in a certain month when he would bring home a lot of sovereigns and buy the children things. Two per cent.! For every hundred pounds' worth of orders, two golden sovereigns of his very own! It seemed too good to be true!

His wife indeed did share with him the comforting joys of this new vista of commercial prosperity. They occupied now two rooms in Camling Town, and Tom had been out so long there was no immediate prospect of a removal. But the rent was now secure and just the barest necessities of life, and everything depended on the two per cent, commission. He was to start on the following Monday, and the intervening days were filled with active preparations. There were shirts to mend, an overcoat to be stitched, a pair of boots to have the heels set up, and three new collars to be bought. These were vital things pertinent to the active propaganda of the bread-winner. Other things were urgent, -a new piece of oil-cloth for the bedroom, some underclothes for the girls, and several small debts-but all these things could wait, at any rate a month or two, till the commissions started coming in. For Mrs. Pinwell herself there never seemed necessities. She always managed to look somehow respectable, and, as Mr. Pinwell once remarked to a neighbor," My wife is a marvel, sir, with a string bag. She always believes in bringing the things home herself. She goes out into the High Street, Camling Town, on a Saturday night, and I assure you, sir, it's surprising what she will bring back. She will make a shilling go further than many of them would half-a-crown. She is a remarkable woman. It surprises me how she manages to bargain, being so unassuming, so diffident, as it were, in the home."

There was nothing, then, missing in the necessary equipment of Mr. Pinwell as he set out with his leather case of samples on the following Monday. It was a cold, bright day, and he enjoyed the exercise of walking. He was not by nature a pushful man and he found the business of calling on people whom he did not know somewhat irksome. Fortunately he was by temperament patient and understanding, and he made allowances when people were rude to him, or kept him waiting indefinitely and then gave him no orders. "It's all in the way of business," he thought as he shuffled out of the shop and sought the next street.

At the end of the first week he explained to his wife:

"You see, my dear, there's a lot of spade-work to be done yet. I 'm afraid Flinders, who had the round before me, must have neglected it disgracefully. It all requires working up again. One has to get to know people, the right people, of course. They seem prejudiced against one like, at first.

"Was that Mr. Flinders who used to—" began Mrs. Pinwell in a whisper.

"Yes, my dear, I 'm afraid he drank. It was a very distressing story, very distressing indeed. They say he drank himself to death. A very clever salesman too-very clever! They tell me he worked this district up splendidly, and then gradually let it go to pieces."

"Dear, dear! I can't think how people do such things!" murmured Mrs. Pin well.

"It was a great recommendation in my case," continued her husband, "that I was a teetotaler. Mr. Hylam made a great point of that. He asked me several times, and read the letter of Judkins & Co. vouching for my honesty and sobriety for a period of twenty-two years. He seemed very pleased about that."

At the end of the first month the orders that Mr. Pinwell had secured for Doll bones were of a negligible character. He felt discouraged—as though conscious of there being something fundamentally wrong in his method of doing business but his wife cheered him by expressing her view that it would probably take months before his initial spade-work would take effect.

He started on his rounds a little earlier after that, and stayed a little later. He became more persistent and more patient. He went back again and again to see people who seemed inaccessible. He tried to be a little more assertive and plausible in his solicitations, but at the end of the second month there was little improvement in his returns, and his commissions amounted to scarcely enough to pay for the new oil-cloth in the sitting-room.

The optimism of Mrs. Pinwell was in no way affected by this failure, but a more alarming note was struck by Mr. Rodney of the "Outer London Department." He told Mr. Pinwell that Mr. Hylam was not at all satisfied with his work so far, and he would have to show greater energy and enterprise during the ensuing month, or the firm would be impelled to try a new traveler for that district, one who could show better results.

Mr. Pinwell was very alarmed. The idea of being "out" again kept him awake at night. It was a very serious thing. He put in longer hours still, and hurried more rapidly between his calls. He increased his stock of samples till they amounted to a very considerable weight. He made desperate appeals for orders, ringing the changes on various ways of expressing himself. But at the end of the next week there was still no improvement on the pages of his order-book. There was one firm in particular who caused him considerable heartburning—Messrs. Carron and Musswell. These were quite the biggest people in the neighborhood, and had five different branches, each doing a prosperous business. Mr. Pinwell for the life of him could not find out how to get into the good graces of this firm. No one seemed to know who bought for them, and he was referred from one person to another, and sent dashing from one branch to another, all to no purpose.

He had one friend who had a small retail business of his own, a Baptist named Senner, who gave him small orders occasionally. He went into Mr. Senner's shop one Friday, and feeling thoroughly tired and discouraged, he poured out his tale of woe to Mr. Senner. Mr. Senner was a large doleful man, to whom the sorrows of others were as balm. He listened to Mr. Pin-well's misfortunes in sympathetic silence, breathing heavily. At the end of the peroration his son entered the shop. He was a white-faced, dissipated-looking young man who wore lavender ties and brushed his hair back.

One might have imagined that he would have been a source of disappointment to Mr. Senner, but quite the contrary was the case. The son had a genius for concealing his vices from his father, and his father had a great opinion of the boy's intelligence and character. He certainly had a faculty of securing orders for his father's business.

On this occasion Mr. Senner turned to his son and said: "Harry, who buys for Carron & Musswell!" The son looked at Mr. Pinwell and fidgeted with his nails. Then he grinned weakly and said:

"Oh, you want to get hold of Clappe." Mr. Pinwell came forward and said:

"Oh, indeed! I 'm really very much obliged to you. It's very kind! Mr. Clappe, you say? Dear me! yes. Thank you very much. I'll go and ask for Mr. Clappe."

And he shook the young man's hand.

The young man continued grinning in rather a superior manner, and at that moment Mr. Senner's attention was attracted by a customer who entered the shop. Mr. Pinwell picked up his bags and went out. He had not gone more than a dozen yards when he became aware of Senner junior at his side. The young man still grinned, and he said:

"I say, you know, it's no good your going to Carron & Musswell's and asking for Clappe. You'll never get hold of him in that way"

"Really!" exclaimed Mr. Pinwell. "Now tell me, what would you suggest!"

The young man sniffed and looked up and down the street, and a curiously leery expression came over his face. Then he said:

"I expect I could fix it for you all right, Pinwell. You'd better come with me into the bar of the ' Three Amazons' after lunch. I'll introduce you. Of course, you know, Mr. Pinwell,—er—you know, business is business. We always like to oblige our friends, and so on-"

He looked at Mr. Pinwell furtively and bit his nails. For the moment Mr. Pin well could not catch the drift of these smiles and suggestions, but he had been in the upholstery line for twenty-seven years, and it suddenly dawned upon him that of course the young man was suggesting that if he introduced him, and business came out of it, he would expect a commission or a bonus. He was quite reasonable. He had a sort of ingrained repugnance to these things himself, but he knew that it was done in business. It was quite a usual thing. Some of the best firms- He took the young man's hand and said:

"Er-of course Mr. Senner, I shall be very pleased to accommodate you. It's -er-only natural, only natural of course. Business is business. Where shall I meet you?"

The appointment was made for the corner of Mulberry Road at half-past two; and at that hour Mr. Pinwell arrived with two heavily laden bags. He walked by the side of the young man down the street, and then crossed over into the High Road. Eight opposite them was a large gaudy public house called "The Three Amazons" and they crossed over to it. A feeling of diffidence and shyness came over Mr. Pinwell. He had only entered a public house on about three occasions in his life, and then under some very stringent business demands, or else to get a bottle of brandy when his wife was very ill.

Nevertheless he followed the young man through a passage and entered the saloon bar, in the corner of which he deposited his bags. The bar was fairly crowded with business men, but there was one figure that by its personality immediately arrested Mr. Pinwell's attention. He was a very big man in a new shiny top-hat with a curl to it. He was leaning heavily against the center of the bar, and was surrounded by three or four other men who seemed to be hanging on his words. He had a large red face and small, dark, expressionless eyes. The skin seemed to be tight and moist, and to bind up his features in inelastic bags, except round the eyes, where it puckered up into dark yellowish layers of flesh. His hands were fat and stiff and blue like the hands of a gouty subject. His gray hair curled slightly under the brim of his hat, and his clothes were ponderously impressive from the silk reveres of his tail coat to the dark-brown spats that covered his square-toed boots. As they entered, this impressive individual looked in their direction and gave young Mr. Senner a faint nod, and then continued his conversation.

"That's Clappe," whispered Mr. Pin-well's cicerone, and dusted the knees of his trousers. He then added:

"We'd better wait a bit."

They stood there in the comer of the bar, and the young man produced a silver cigarette-case and offered its contents to Mr. Pinwell, an overt act of kindness which that gentleman appreciated but did not take advantage of. They waited there twenty minutes before an opportunity presented itself of making any approach to the great man. But in the meantime Mr. Pinwell watched the conversation with considerable interest. The four men stood very close together, smoking, and speaking in thick whispers. He was alarmed at moments by the way in which one would hold a glass of whisky-and-water at a perilous angle over the waistcoat of another, while fumbling with a cigarette in the unoccupied hand. He could not hear the conversation, but occasional sentences reached him: "It's the cheapest line there is." "Here! I tell you where you can get—" "D'you know what they paid last year?"

"I 'ad 'im by the short 'airs that time." "'E says to me—"

It occurred to Mr. Pinwell that there was something distressing about this scene, something repelling and distasteful, but he consoled himself with the reflection that after all business had to be conducted somehow. Money had to be made to pay for the streets and the lamp-posts, and the public baths and the battleships. "Business is not always pleasant," he reflected, "but it has to be done."

At the end of twenty minutes two of the men went away and left Mr. Clappe talking apathetically to the remaining man.

"Now's our chance," said Senner junior, and he walked across the bar. He seized on a lull in the conversation to step forward and touch Mr. Clappe on the arm.

"Er-excuse me, Mr. Clappe," he said. "This is my friend Mr. Pinwell, of Dollbones. "

The big man glanced from Senner junior to Mr. Pinwell and gave that gentleman an almost imperceptible nod. He then sighed, breathed heavily, and took a long drink from the glass in front of him.

"I'm very pleased to meet you, Mr. Clappe," said Pinwell nervously. "I've heard about you. I 'm with Dollbones, you know, the Dollbones. We have-er—several very good lines just now."

The great Clappe fixed him with his lugubrious eyes and suddenly said in a thick voice:

"What'll you drink?''

It is curious that Mr. Pinwell with all his experience should have been taken back by this hospitable request. He stammered and said:

"Oh! thank you very much, sir. I don't think I'll-at least, I'll have-er-a lime-juice and soda."

And then Mr. Clappe behaved in a very extraordinary way. An expression of utter, dejection came over his face. He puffed his cheeks out and suddenly muttered" Oh, my God!"

And then he rolled round and deliberately turned his back on Mr. Pinwell and his friend! It was a very trying moment. Mr. Pinwell was at his wit's end how to act, and Senner junior did not help him in any way. On the contrary he seemed to be taking Mr. Clappe's side. He gave a sort of snigger of disgust, and called across the bar in a jaunty voice:

"Johnny Walker and soda, please, Miss Parritt."

Mr. Pinwell gaped ineffectually at the back of the great man, and hesitated whether to make any further advance. But he was relieved of the necessity of coming to a decision by the act of Mr. Clappe himself, who slowly drained the remnants of refreshment in his glass, and then walked heavily out of the bar, without looking round.

In the meantime young Senner had acquired his drink, and was feverishly tapping the end of a cigarette on the rail. He took a long drink and spluttered slightly, and then, turning on Mr. Pinwell, he said:

"What particular brand of blankety fool are you?"

"I beg your pardon?" exclaimed Mr. Pinwell, amazed.

"I tell you," said the young man, "you're a particular type of blankety fool. You've missed the chance of yer life I Don't you know when a man like Clappe asks yer to have a drink yer a blankety fool not to? D' you know that man places thousands and thousands of pounds a year for Carron & Musswell? Thousands, I tell yer! It don't matter to 'im where he places the orders. He puts it all out among 'is pals. You 'ad a chance of being a pal, and you've muffed it!"

"But—but—but—" spluttered Mr. Pin-well." I really—I—had no idea. I said I would have a drink. It was only that I ordered a—er—non-alcoholic drink. I really can't—"

"Psaugh!"

Young Mr. Senner swirled the whisky round in his glass and drank it at a gulp. Then he muttered: "Gawd! Asking Clappe for a lime-juice and soda!"

Mr. Pinwell thought about this meditatively. He wondered whether he had been in the wrong. After all, people all had their notions of the way to conduct business. Business was a very big thing. It had "evolved"—that was the word!—evolved out of all sorts of complicated social conditions, supply and demand, and so on. A man perhaps who had been in the habit of taking alcoholic refreshment and expecting others to—it might perhaps be difficult for him to understand.

"Don't you never drink!" suddenly exclaimed Mr. Senner.

"I—er—occasionally have a glass of stout," murmured Mr. Pinwell. "Last Christmas my wife's sister brought us a bottle of canary sac. I have no particular taste for—er—things of this sort-"

"Anyway," said Mr. Senner, "you're not under any bally pledge?"

"Oh, dear me, no!" exclaimed Mr. Pin-well.

"Well, then," answered his youthful adviser. "I should advise you next time Clappe or any one like him asks you to have a drink, lap it up like a poodle and stand him a quick one in return."

Mr. Pinwell surveyed his friend over the rim of his glasses, and thought for some minutes. Then he said:

"I 'm afraid Mr. Clappe is not likely to ask me to have a drink again." But the young man of precocious experience answered:

"If you come in here to-morrer, I'll bet yer he'll have forgotten who you are"

It was all a very astounding experience, and that night in- bed Mr. Pinwell gave the matter long and serious consideration. If his circumstances had been normal he would have hardly thought about it for five consecutive minutes, but his circumstances were anything but normal. They were somewhat desperate. He was on his last month's trial. If he should be out again! ... Both the children wanted new clothes, and Eileen's boots were all to pieces. And then there was that bill of Batson's for three pounds seventeen shillings, for which payment was demanded by the seventeenth; there were other bills less urgent perhaps but-the little man kept turning restlessly in bed and even in his sleep he made febrile calculations.

It must be acknowledged that the result of Mr. Pinwell's nocturnal meditations tended to loosen certain moral tendencies in himself. He set out on the morrow in a peculiarly equivocal frame of mind, wavering between conflicting impulses, but already predisposed to temporize with his conscience if by so doing he could advance what he considered to be the larger issues of business considerations. These first concessions, curiously enough, were not made at the instance of the great Mr. Clappe, however, but at that of a certain Mr. Cherish whom he met during that day. He was a breezy, amiable person, and the manager of the International Hardwood Company. He was just going out to lunch as Mr. Pinwell called, and being in a particularly buoyant mood, owing to a successful business deal, he took hold of our hero's arm and drew him into the street. As they walked along he asked what it was that Pinwell wanted, and that gentleman immediately expatiated on the virtues of the goods he had at his disposal. While talking he found himself almost unconsciously led into the bar of a public-house called "The Queen of Roumania." And when asked by Mr. Cherish," What he was going to have," a sudden desperate instinct of adventure came over him, and he called for whisky. When it was brought he drank it in little sips, and thought it the most detestable drink he had ever tasted. But he determined to see the matter through, and salved his conscience with the reflection that it was just 'an the way of business." He certainly had to acknowledge that after drinking it he felt a certain elevated sense of assurance. He talked to Mr. Cherish quite unselfconsciously and listened to him with concentrated attention. This mental attitude was quickened by the discovery that Mr. Cherish was actually in need of certain embroideries that Dollbones were in a position to supply. It would be quite a big order. He promised to bring samples of the embroideries on the following day, and took his departure. During the afternoon he felt a sudden reaction from the whisky and was very tired. He went home early, complaining to his wife of a bad headache, as though something had disagreed with him."

Nevertheless the prospect of securing the order for the embroideries excited him considerably, and he went so far as to tell her that he hoped things were soon going to take a tum for the better. He arrived at his appointment the next day to the minute, carrying a very heavy valise stuffed with machine embroideries. He was kept waiting by Mr. Cherish for nearly an hour, and was then ushered into his presence. Mr. Cherish was still in a very jovial mood and had another gentleman with him. He shook Mr.

Pinwell's hand and immediately told him three obscene stories that he had just heard-Mr. Cherish was reputed to have the largest repertoire of obscene stories in the trade-and the other gentleman also told two. Pinwell laughed at them to the best of his ability, although they did not appear to him to be particularly humorous. He then felt peculiarly uncomfortable in that for the life of him he could not think of a story in reply. He never could remember these stories. So he opened his valise and displayed the tapestries. The other two gentlemen took a desultory interest in them as tapestries, but a rapacious interest in them as regards value. They were figured tapestries and the price was four pounds seventeen and sixpence a yard. Mr. Cherish mentioned casually that they would want about seventy yards. And then Mr. Pin-well made the rapidest mental calculation he had ever made in his life. Seventy yards at £4,17s. 6d. would be £341,55s. which, at two per cent, would mean just on seven pounds for himself! It was dazzling! Seven gold sovereigns! However, the order was not yet given. The two gentlemen talked about it at some length, and looked up other quotations. At last Mr. Cherish said:

"Well, I think we'll go and see what the 'Queen of Roumania' has got up her sleeve."

Mr. Pinwell and the other gentleman laughed, and they all went out. Mr. Pin well dreaded the prospect of drinking more whisky, but-seven golden sovereigns! enough to pay that bill of Batson's and to buy the children all the clothes they wanted! He knew in any case the etiquette of the trade, and when they arrived in the resplendent bar it was he who insisted on ordering "three Scotch whiskies and a split soda." On the arrival of these regenerating beverages the other two gentlemen resumed their sequence of improper stories. And it was just after the glasses had been re-charged at the instance of Mr. Cherish that he suddenly recollected a story he had heard nearly twenty years ago. It was a disgusting story, and it had impressed itself on his memory for the reason that it struck him when he heard it as being so incredibly vulgar that he could not understand how any one could appreciate it. But as he neared the end of his second glass of whisky it suddenly flashed into his mind that here was the story that Mr. Cherish and his friend would like. He had by this time arrived at an enviable state of unselfconsciousness, and he told the story as well as he had ever told anything in his life. The result amazed him.

The other two gentlemen roared with laughter, and Mr. Cherish tilted his hat back and slapped his leg.

"Gawd's truth! that's a damn good story, Pinwell!" he cried out several times. Other people came into the bar, and Mr. Pinwell found himself something of a hero. Every one seemed to know Mr. Cherish, and he introduced him, and on several occasions said, "I say, Pinwell, tell Mr. Watson that story about the sea captain."

The story was an unqualified success, and seemed in some way to endear him to Mr. Cherish. That gentleman became more confidential and confiding, and they talked about business.

Mr. Pinwell believed he drank four whiskies-and-sodas that afternoon. In any case, he arrived home feeling very bilious and ill. He told his wife he had felt faint, and had taken some brandy+" Thank heaven," he thought, "she doesn't know the difference in smell between brandy and whisky!" He said he would go to bed at once, he thought, and he kissed her in rather a maudlin fashion, and said he knew she would be glad to hear that he had that afternoon taken an order for £341—that would mean nearly seven pounds to them I Enough to buy clothes for the children and pay Batson's bill; he laughed a little hysterically after that, and rolled into bed.

On the following day he was very unwell and unable to get up, and Mrs. Pinwell wrote to the firm and explained that her husband had got his feet wet on his rounds and had contracted a chill. She also inclosed his order-book.

It was three days before he was well enough to resume his rounds, and then he avoided the company of Mr. Cherish and set out on a pilgrimage to the meaner parts of the district. But the orders there seemed few and far between, and a feeling of depression came over him.

On the 1st of the month he was bidden to the presence of Mr. Rodney. That gentleman said that the firm was still dissatisfied with his efforts, but on the strength of the order he had secured from the International Hardwood Co. they were willing to keep him on for another month's trial. But unless at the end of that time he had secured further orders of a similar nature, he must consider his engagement at an end.

It would be tedious and extremely disconcerting to follow the precise movements of Thomas Pinwell during the ensuing four Weeks. It need only be said that, utterly discouraged by his lonely peregrinations in the paths of honest effort, he eventually once more sought the society of young Mr. Senner and Mr. Cherish. In their company he discovered what might be called "a cheering fluidity." He found that whisky made him so ill that he simply could not drink it, but he drank ale, stout, brandy, and gin. None of these things agreed with him, but he found that by drinking as little as possible and ringing the changes on them he could just manage to keep going. The direct result of this moral defection was that his circle of business acquaintances increased at an enormous rate. He gradually got to know the right place and the right hour to catch the right people. His efforts on behalf of Messrs. Dollbones during the following three months were eminently satisfactory, and his own commissions amounted to no mean sum. Neither was his conscience seriously affected by this change of habit. He considered it an inevitable development of his own active progress '4n the way of business." The very word "business" had a peculiarly mesmerizing effect upon him. It was a fetish. He looked upon it as an acolyte might look upon the dogma of some faith he blindly believed in.

He believed that people were in some mysterious way pale adjuncts to the idea that whatever happens," Business" must go on. He would stand in the corner of the bar of "The Queen of Boumania" and look across the street at the Camling Town public wash-houses, a mid-Victorian Gothic building in stucco and red brick, and then, turning his mild watery eyes towards Senner junior, he would say:

"It's a wonderful thing-business, you know, Mr. Senner, a very wonderful thing indeed. Now look at the wash-houses!

They simply have been the result of business. No progress is made, nothing is done except through business. If it weren't for business we should all be Barbarians." And then he would take a little sip at the gin-and-water in front of him.

After copious trials he found that gin affected him less than any of the other drinks, so he stuck to that. He did not like it, but he found that people simply would not do business with him in Camling Town unless he drank and stood drinks. It was very trying, and the most trying part was the necessity of concealing these aberrations from his wife. When he first started he was conscious that he often returned home smelling of the disgusting stuff. He tried cloves, but they were not very effective. Then one day he had a brilliant inspiration. He was unwell again. It happened very often now-at least once a week-and the doctor gave him some medicine. Then it occurred to him that medicine might smell like anything else. He would keep up the medicine. His wife was very unsuspecting. He hated deceiving her. He had never deceived her about anything, but he thought, "Women don't understand business. It is for her benefit that I take it."

Sunday was a great joy to him. He would take the children out for a walk in the morning while his wife cooked the dinner. In the afternoon he would have a nap; but the greatest luxury of the day seemed to him that he need drink nothing except water.

At the end of six months there came a proud day when Mr. Rodney informed him that Mr. Hylam was quite satisfied with his progress, and his ordinary salary was raised to two pounds. It was summertime, and the accumulation of his commissions justified the family moving into larger rooms, one of which was to be a bathroom. But Mr. Pinwell was beginning to feel his health very much affected, and he looked forward with intense avidity to the two weeks' holiday which was his due in September. In July he achieved a great triumph. He met and got into the good graces of the great Mr. Clappe. As Senner junior predicted, that gentleman had quite forgotten their previous meeting, and it happened in the company of the good Mr. Cherish. They all met in the bar of "The Cormorant," and after several drinks Cherish said:

"I say, Pinwell, tell Mr. Clappe that story about the sea captain!"

Mr. Pinwell complied, and when he had finished he saw the shiny bags of flesh on Mr. Clappe 's face shaking. He was evidently very much amused, although his eyes looked hard and tired. He said hoarsely:

"Damn good! What's yours?"

Mr. Pinwell did not fail on this occasion, and asked for some gin. And directly he noticed that the great man's glass was nearly empty, he insisted on ordering some more all round. He found Mr. Clappe an expensive client. He drank prodigiously, in a splendid nonchalant manner, hardly noticing it, or taking any interest in who paid for it. It took Mr. Pinwell several weeks, and cost him the price of several whole bottles of whisky, before he became sufficiently established in favor to solicit orders. But once having arrived there, the rest was easy, for Mr. Clappe had the reputation of being '4oyal to his pals," and he had the power of placing very large orders.

There came a day when Mr. Pinwell received an order for over eight hundred pounds' worth of goods, and for the first time in his life he got very drunk. He arrived home in a cab very late at night and was just conscious enough to tell his wife that he had been taken ill, and some one had given him some brandy, and it had gone to his head. She helped him to bed, and seemed rather surprised and alarmed.

On the following day he was very ill, and a doctor was sent for. He examined him carefully, and looked stern. Out in the hall he said to Mrs. Pinwell:

"Excuse me, Mrs. Pinwell, but does your husband drink rather a lot?" "Drink!" exclaimed the lady. "My Tom? ... Why, he's practically a teetotaler."

The doctor looked at her thoughtfully and murmured," Oh!" Then, as he turned to go, he said:

"Well, we'll pull him through this, I hope, but he must be very careful. You must advise him never to touch alcohol in any form. It's poison to him," and he left Mrs. Pinwell speechless with indignation.

Mr. Pinwell's illness proved more obstinate than was anticipated, and it was some weeks before he was well enough to get about. When he arrived at that stage the firm of Dollbones were considerate enough to suggest that he might take his holiday earlier than had been arranged, and go away at once.

Consequently, on a certain fine morning in August, Mr. and Mrs. Pinwell, with the two children, set out for a fortnight's holiday to Heme Bay. The firm paid his salary while he was away, and in addition he had now nearly thirty-five pounds in the bank, and all his debts were paid. It was many years since the family had been in such an affluent position, and everything pointed to the prospect of a joyous and beneficial time. And so indeed, to a large extent, it was. Mr. Pinwell felt very shaky when he arrived, and he spent most of his time sitting in a deck chair on the sands, watching the children, while his wife sat on the sands by his side, sewing. The fresh breezes from the Channel made him very sleepy at first, but he gradually got used to them. It was extremely pleasant sitting there listening to the waves breaking on the shore and watching the white sails of yachts gliding hither and thither; very pleasant and very refreshing. It was only after some days that when he was left alone a certain moroseness came over him. He could not explain this to himself; it seemed so unreasonable. But he felt a curious and restless desire and an irritability. These moods became more pronounced as the week advanced, in spite of the fact that his strength returned to him. He had moods when he wished to be alone and the children tired him.

On the fifth day, he and his wife were strolling up from the beach late in the afternoon, and they were nearing their lodgings when he suddenly said:

"I think I'll just stroll round and get a paper."

"Oh! Shall I come with you?" his wife asked.

"No, no, my dear. Don't. Er—I'll just stroll round by myself-"

He seemed so anxious to go by himself that she did not insist, and he sauntered round the corner. He looked back to see that she had gone in, and then he walked rather more quickly round into the High Street. He hummed to himself and glanced rather furtively at the contents of the newspaper bills, then, after looking up and down the street, he suddenly darted into the saloon bar of the principal hotel. ...

After his second glass of gin-and-water a feeling of comfortable security crept over him. After all, it was a very ingratiating atmosphere this, ingratiating and sociable. He glanced round the bar and carried on a brief but formal conversation with a florid individual standing near him. He hesitated for a moment whether he would tell him the story about the sea captain, but on second thoughts decided to reserve it to a more intimate occasion. Besides, he must not be away long.

After that it became a habit with Mr. Pinwell for the rest of the holiday for him at some time during the day, and occasionally twice or three times during the day, to "go for a stroll round by himself." His wife never for one moment suspected the purpose of these wanderings, though she was informed that he was taking another bottle of the medicine.

When they returned to town Mr. Pinwell certainly seemed better and more eager about his work. It may be that he had the measure of his constitution more under control. He knew what was the least damaging drink he could take, and he knew how much he dare consume without immediately disastrous results. He gradually became a well-known habitue of all the best-known saloon bars in the neighborhood of his rounds. His character altered. He always remained mild and unassertive, but his face became pinched and thin, and he began to enjoy the reputation of being a "knowing one." He did not make a fortune in his solicitations for orders for gimp, trimmings, buttons, and embroidery, but he certainly earned a very fair competence. In two years' time he was entirely intimate with every buyer of importance in the Camling Town district and out as far as the "Teck Arms" at Highgate. The family still occupied the larger rooms (with the bathroom) that they had moved to, and both the girls attended the Camling Town Collegiate School for Girls, and showed every promise of being worthy and attractive members of society.

It was not till the end of the second year that two events following rapidly on each other's heels tended to disturb the normal conditions of the Pinwell family. A letter arrived one day from a lawyer.
It appeared that a brother of Mr. Pinwell's whom he had not seen for twelve years, and who had owned a farm in Northamptonshire, had died intestate. He was not married, and Tom Pinwell was his only living relative. Under the circumstances he inherited the whole of his brother's property.

When this had been assessed it was proved to be worth £140 per year. Needless to say this news brought great joy to the traveler's family. Visions of great splendor opened out before them, wealth, comfort, security. The day after the settlement was made, Tom Pinwell entertained Mr. Cherish, Mr. Clappe, and a few others of his friends to a supper at "The Queen of Roumania," and the next day he was taken Very ill. He lay in a critical state for ten days, nursed with a sort of feline intensity by his wife. The doctor then said that he might recover-he was a different doctor to the one who had so exasperated Mrs. Pinwell with his outrageous suggestions- but that he would be an invalid all his life. He would have to live on special food and must not touch either sweets or alcohol in any form.

On a certain evening Mr. Pinwell showed traces of convalescence and was allowed to sit up in bed. His wife as usual sat by his bedside, knitting. He seemed more cheerful than he had ever been before, and Mrs. Pinwell took the opportunity of saying:

"What a blessing it is, dear, about this money!"

"Yes, dear," answered her spouse.

"Do you know, Tom," she said suddenly, "there is a thing I've Wanted to do all my life. And now perhaps is the opportunity."

"What is that, my dear?"

"To go and live in the country."

"Yes, dear."

"Think of it! When you're better, we can go and get a little cottage somewhere, with a bit of a garden, you know-grow our own vegetables and that. You can live fine in some parts of the country for £140 a year. You'll be able to give up this nasty tiring old business. It'll be lovely."

"Yes, my dear."

Mr. Pinwell's voice sounded rather faint, and she busied herself with his beef tea. Nothing more was said about the idea that night. But gradually, as he got stronger, Mrs. Pinwell enlarged on the idea. She talked about the flowers they could grow, and the economy of having your own fowls and potatoes. It would have to be right in the country, but not too far from a village or town, so that the girls could continue their schooling and meet other girls. To all of this Mr. Pinwell agreed faintly, and he even made a suggestion that he thought Surrey was nicer than Buckinghamshire.

Mr. Pinwell was confined to his bedroom for nearly two months. And then one day a letter came from Messrs. Dollbones. It was to say that in view of the short time that Mr. Pinwell had been in their service they could not see their way to continue paying his salary after the end of the month, unless he were well enough to continue his work.

Mrs. Pinwell said:

"No, and they needn't continue to pay it at all, for all we care!"

A troubled look came over her husband's face, and he said:

"Um-they've treated me very well, Emma, very well indeed. There's many firms don't pay their employees at all when they're ill."

"Well then, they jolly well ought to," answered Mrs. Pinwell. "People get ill through doing the firm's work."

Mr. Pinwell sniffed. It was the one subject upon which he and his wife were inclined to differ. Mrs. Pinwell did not understand business; she had no reverence for it.

By the end of the month Mr. Pinwell was up again and going for short walks up and down the street. One day he said:

"Let me see, my dear-next Thursday is the first of the new month, isn't it?" "Yes," answered Mrs. Pinwell. "And thank goodness you haven't got to go back to that horrid old business!">

Mr. Pinwell said nothing at the time, but a few hours later he said:

"Er-I've been thinking, my dear. I rather think I ought perhaps to-er-to try and see if I could go for a little while on Thursday. You see, the firm have treated me very generously, very generously indeed-and-er-business is business"

"What does it matter?" answered his wife. "I'm sure they've got some one else doing your job by now. Besides, you're not strong enough."

Mr. Pinwell fidgeted with his watch-chain and walked up the street. During the next two days Mrs. Pinwell could tell that he was fretting. He seemed distracted and inclined to be irritable. He gave demonstrations of his walking powers and stayed out longer and moved more quickly. He got into such a state on the Wednesday evening, that in a weak moment Mrs. Pinwell made the mistake of her life.

She agreed that he might try and go the next day just for an hour or so, but he was to come home directly he felt tired.

Tom started out on the Thursday morning, and he seemed in a great state of elation. In spite of his weakness he insisted on taking one of his bags of samples. He walked more quickly down the street than she had seen him walk for a long time. Mrs. Pinwell then turned to her household duties. She was disappointed, but not entirely surprised, that her husband did not come home to lunch, but at half-past three a sudden curious feeling of alarm came over her. She tried to reason with herself that it was all nonsense; nothing had happened, Tom was a little late-that was all. But her reason quailed before some more insidious sense of calamity. The children came home from school at a quarter-past four, and still he had not returned. She gave them their tea and somehow their gay chatter irritated her for the first time. She would not convey to them her sense of fear. She washed up the tea-things and busied herself in the house.

It was a quarter to six when Tom came home. He staggered into the hall. His eyes had a strange look she had not seen before. He was trembling violently. She did not ask any questions. She took his arm and led him into the bedroom and untied his collar and tie. He lay on the bed and his teeth chattered. She got him a hot-water bottle and gradually undressed him. Then she sent one of the girls for the doctor.

In the meantime he started talking incoherently, although he repeated on one or two occasions, "I've taken another bottle of the medicine, Emm'."

The doctor was on duty in the surgery when the child called, and he did not come round till half-past eight.

When he looked at Pinwell and took his pulse, he said: "What's he been doing?"

"He's been out," said Mrs. Pinwell. "He said he'd taken another bottle of the medicine."

"Medicine? what medicine?" The doctor seemed to examine the lips of the sick man very closely, then he shook his head. He turned to Mrs. Pinwell as though he were going to make a statement, then he changed his mind. It did not require any great astuteness to determine from the doctor's face that the case was critical. He gave the patient a powder, and after a few instructions to Mrs. Pinwell he went, and said he would return later in 'he evening. After the doctor had gone, Mr. Pinwell was delirious for an hour, and then he sank into a deep sleep. The doctor returned just after eleven. He examined him and said that nothing more could be done that night. He would return in the morning. In the meantime, if things took a more definite turn, they could send for him.

Tom Pinwell lay unconscious for nearly twenty-four hours, sometimes mumbling feverishly, at other times falling into a deep coma. But suddenly, late on the following evening, he seemed to alter. His face cleared, and he sighed peacefully. Mrs. Pinwell noticed the change and she went up close to the bed. He looked at her and said suddenly:

"I don't think it would do, my dear, to go and live in the country." "No, no, dear; all right. We'll live where you like."

"You see," he said after a pause," business has to be gone through .... There was Judkins & Cd., they treated me very fair, then they went bankrupt. It was very unfortunate, very unfortunate indeed .... I wouldn't like these people-what's their name, Emma? ... "

"Dollbones."

"Ah, yes, Dollbones! ... Dollbones. No, I wouldn't like them to think I'd let them in like. Just because I had a little money.... It's a very serious thing business ... "

Mr. Pinwell seemed about to say something, but he smiled instead and looked up at the ceiling. He became very still after that, and Mrs. Pinwell placed a book so that the candle-light should not shine on his face. All through the night she sat there watching and doing the little things the doctor had told her to. But he was very still. Once he sighed, and on another occasion she thought he said:

hot-water bottle and gradually undressed him. Then she sent one of the girls for the doctor.

In the meantime he started talking incoherently, although he repeated on one or two occasions, "I've taken another bottle of the medicine, Emm'."

The doctor was on duty in the surgery when the child called, and he did not come round till half-past eight.

When he looked at Pinwell and took his pulse, he said: "What's he been doing?"

"He's been out," said Mrs. Pinwell. "He said he'd taken another bottle of the medicine."

"Medicine? what medicine?" The doctor seemed to examine the lips of the sick man very closely, then he shook his head. He turned to Mrs. Pinwell as though he were going to make a statement, then he changed his mind. It did not require any great astuteness to determine from the doctor's face that the case was critical. He gave the patient a powder, and after a few instructions to Mrs. Pinwell he went, and said he would return later in 'he evening. After the doctor had gone, Mr. Pinwell was delirious for an hour, and then he sank into a deep sleep. The doctor returned just after eleven. He examined him and said that nothing more could be done that night. He would return in the morning. In the meantime, if things took a more definite tum, they could send for him.

Tom Pinwell lay unconscious for nearly twenty-four hours, sometimes mumbling feverishly, at other times falling into a deep coma. But suddenly, late on the following evening, he seemed to alter. His face cleared, and he sighed peacefully. Mrs. Pinwell noticed the change and she went up close to the bed. He looked at her and said suddenly:

"I don't think it would do, my dear, to go and live in the country." "No, no, dear; all right. We'll live where you like."

"You see," he said after a pause," business has to be gone through .... There was Judkins & Cd., they treated me very fair, then they went bankrupt. It was very unfortunate, very unfortunate indeed .... I wouldn't like these people-what's their name, Emma? ... "

"Dollbones."

"Ah, yes, Dollbones! ... Dollbones. No, I wouldn't like them to think I'd let them in like. Just because I had a little money.... It's a very serious thing business ... "

Mr. Pinwell seemed about to say something, but he smiled instead and looked up at the ceiling. He became very still after that, and Mrs. Pinwell placed a book so that the candle-light should not shine on his face. All through the night she sat there watching and doing the little things the doctor had told her to. But he was very still. Once he sighed, and on another occasion she thought he said:

"That was very amusin' about that invoice of Barrel and Beelswright, Mr. Cherish . . . oh, dear me!"

About dawn, thoroughly exhausted with her vigil, Mrs. Pinwell fell into a fitful sleep, sitting up in her chair. She only slept for a few minutes, and then awakened with a start. The short end of candle was spluttering in its socket, and its light was contending with the cold blue glimmer of the early day. She shivered, her frame racked by physical fatigue, and her mind benumbed by the incredible stillness of the little room.

"Consequently, ladies and gentlemen, after placing £17,500 in the reserve fund, for the reasons which I have indicated to you, I feel justified in recommending a dividend of 12 per cent, on the ordinary shares."

The big man with the square chin dabbed his forehead with his handkerchief and took a sip of water as he resumed his seat. A faint murmur of approval and applause ran round the room; papers rustled, and people spoke in low, breathless voices. Twelve and a half per cent! It was a good dividend, a very good dividend! A hundred different brains visualized rapidly what it meant to them personally. To some it meant a few extra luxuries, to others comforts, and to some a distinct social advance. If Dollbones could only keep this up!

Sir Arthur Schelling was seconding the adoption of this report, but it was a mere formality. No one took any interest in the white-haired financier, except to nudge each other and say, "That's Schelling. They say he's worth half a million." It was a curiously placid meeting, there was no criticism, and every one seemed on the best of terms. It broke up, and the shareholders dispersed into little knots, or scattered to spread the good news that Dollbones were paying twelve and a half per cent.

Sir Arthur took the chairman's hand and murmured:

"I must congratulate you, Hylam. An excellent report!"

The large man almost blushed with pleasure, and said:

"It's very kind of you, Sir Arthur. Are you lunching in town?"

"I was going to suggest that you lunch with me at the Carlton. I have my car here."

"Oh! thank you very much. I shall be delighted."

Mr. Hylam turned and gave a few instructions to his lawyer and his private secretary, and handed various papers to each; then he followed his host out of the Cannon Street Hotel.

They got into the great car, and each man lighted a well-merited cigar. As they drove through the city, Sir Arthur discussed a few details of the balance-sheet, and then added:

"I really think you have shown a remarkable genius of organization in conducting this business, Hylam. It is a business which I should imagine requires considerable technical knowledge and great—er—tact."

Mr. Hylam laughed deprecatingly and muttered:

"Oh, we have our little difficulties!" He puffed at his cigar and looked out of the window.

"So many—er—varieties of employees, I should imagine?" said Sir Arthur.

"Yes, you're right, sir. There are varieties. I've had a lot of difficulty with the travelers this year." He gave a vicious puff at his cigar and stamped on the ash on the floor, and suddenly exclaimed:

"Drunken swine!"

Sir Arthur readjusted his gold-rimmed pince-nez and looked at his friend.

"Is that so indeed?"

"Yes," answered Mr. Hylam. "I don't know how it is. They nearly all drink. In one district alone, I've had two travelers practically drink themselves to death, one after the other."

"I'm very distressed to hear that," said Sir Arthur; "very distressed. It's a very great social evil. My wife, as you may know, is on a board of directorship of the Blue Bib and Evangelists. They do a lot of good work. They have a branch in Camling Town. They have pleasant evenings, you know—cocoa and bagatelle, and so on; and lectures on Sunday. But, I don't know, it doesn't seem to eradicate the evil."

"No; I'm afraid it's in the blood with many of them," said the managing director.

"Yes, that's very true. I often tell my wife I'm afraid she wastes her time. It seems inexplicable. I can't see why they should do it. What satisfaction can it be to—er—drink to excess? And then it must hamper them so in the prosecution of their work. It seems in a way so—ungrateful, to the people who employ them, I mean. Ah! here we are at the Carlton! Champneys, come back for me at—er—three thirty. Yes, it's a great social evil, a very great social evil indeed!"

Stacy Aumonier – A Short Biography

Stacy Aumonier was born at Hampstead Road near Regent's Park, London on 31st March 1877.

He came from a family with a strong and sustained tradition in the visual arts; sculptors and painters.

In 1890 the teenage Aumonier attended Cranleigh School in Surrey. Although he would later write critically about English public schools (with articles for the London Evening Standard and New York Times) in how they tried to impose conformity on students, records indicate that he integrated well into Cranleigh. Aumonier was a passionate cricket player, belonged to the Literary and Debating Society, and, in his final year, became a prefect.

On leaving school it seemed the family tradition of the visual arts would be his career path. In particular his early talents were that of a landscape painter. He exhibited paintings at the Royal Academy in 1902 and 1903, and 1908. An exhibition of his work would later be held at the Goupil Gallery in London in 1911.

In 1907 he married the international concert pianist, Gertrude Peppercorn, at West Horsley in Surrey. She herself was the daughter of a landscape painter (Arthur Douglas Peppercorn, occasionally cited as 'the English Corot'.) A son, Timothy, was born in 1921.

A year after his marriage, Aumonier began a brief career in a second branch of the arts at which he enjoyed outstanding success—as a stage performer writing and performing his own sketches.

The Observer newspaper commented that "...the stage lost in him a real and rare genius, he could walk out alone before any audience, from the simplest to the most sophisticated, and make it laugh or cry at will."

In 1915, Aumonier published a short story 'The Friends' which was well received (and voted one of the best short stories of 1915 by the Boston Magazine, Transcript).

Despite his age being 40 in 1917 he was called up for service in World War I. He began as a private in the Army Pay Corps, and then transferred as a draughtsman in the Ministry of National Service.

By now he had four books published—two novels and two books of short stories—and his occupation is recorded with the Army Medical Board as 'author.'

In the mid-1920s, Aumonier received the shattering diagnosis that he had contracted tuberculosis. In the last few years of his life, he would spend long spells in various sanatoria, some better than others. In a letter to his friend, Rebecca West, written shortly before his death, he described the debilitating conditions in a sanatorium in Norfolk during the winter of 1927, where the dampness was so severe that a newspaper left beside the bed would feel "sodden to the touch in the morning."

Shortly before his death, Stacy Aumonier sought treatment in Switzerland, but died of the disease in Clinique La Prairie at Clarens beside Lake Geneva on 21st December 1928. He was 55.

Whilst Aumonier's works are now slowly coming back into circulation at the time of his death his works were extremely popular and his loss was a profound tragedy for literary society.

The chief fiction critic of The Observer, Gerald Gould wrote: "His gifts were almost fantastically various; they embraced all the arts; but it was the charm and generosity of his personality which made him— what he unquestionably was—one of the most popular men of his generation." It went on: "The things he wrote will be remembered when the company of his friends (no man had more friends, or more devoted and admiring) are with him in the grave; but just now, to those who knew him, the thing most vividly present is the charm and wisdom of the man they knew."

Of his general appearance and manner Gerald Cumberland gives us this interesting set of observations: "A distinguished man, this—distinguished both in mind and appearance. Self-conscious. Perhaps. Why not? His hair is worn a trifle long, and it is arranged so that his fine forehead, broad and high, may be fully revealed. Round his neck is a very high collar and a modern stock. When in repose, his face has a look of shy eagerness; his quick eyes glance here and there gathering a thousand impressions to be stored up in his brain. It is the face of a man extremely sensitive to external stimulus; one feels that his brain works not only rapidly, but with great accuracy. And at heart, he takes himself and his work seriously, though he likes on occasion to pretend that he is only a philanderer."

In literary terms Aumonier was amongst the best short story writers these shores have produced.

The Nobel Prize winning author John Galsworthy called him "A real master of the short story. The first essential in a short-story writer is the power of interesting sentence by sentence. Aumonier had this power in prime degree. You do not have to 'get into' his stories. He is especially notable for investing his figures with the breadth of life within a few sentences." Galsworthy asserted that Aumonier "is never heavy, never boring, never really trivial; interested himself, he keeps us interested. At the back of his tales, there is belief in life and a philosophy of life, and of how many short story writers can that be said? ...He follows no fashion and no school. He is always himself. And can't he write? Ah! Far better than far more pretentious writers. Nothing escapes his eye, but he describes without affectation or redundancy, and you sense in him a feeling for beauty that is never obtruded. He gets values right, and that is to say nearly everything. The easeful fidelity of his style has militated against his reputation in these somewhat posturing times. But his shade may rest in peace, for in this volume, at least he will outlive nearly all the writers of his day." In summing his up Galsworthy suggested that, through his stories, he would "outlive all the writers of his day."

James Hilton (author of Goodbye, Mr Chips and Lost Horizon) said "I think his very best works ought to be included in any anthology of the best short stories ever written." He cited 'The Octave of Jealously' as his favourite short story for the March 1939 edition of Good Housekeeping saying it was a "bitterly brilliant tale."

Rebecca West said of his writing in 1922 that his ability to blend reality with the imaginary was "the envy of all artists."

Stacy Aumonier – A Concise Bibliography

More than 87 short stories in more than 25 magazines, and in 6 volumes published during Aumonier's lifetime.

Among more than 20 other magazines, his work appeared in Argosy Magazine, John O' London's Weekly, The Strand Magazine and The Saturday Evening Post, as well as being anthologized, and adapted for film and television.

Short Story Collections

The Golden Windmill & Other Stories (1921)
The Friends & Other Stories (1917)
Miss Bracegirdle & Other Stories (1923)

Novels

Olga Bardel (1916)
Three Bars Interval (1917)
Just Outside (1917)
The Querrils (1919)
One After Another (1920)
Heartbeat (1922)

Other Works

A volume of 14 Character Studies: Odd Fish (1923)

A volume of 15 Essays: Essays of Today and Yesterday (1926)